When the Sea Gives Up Its Dead

When the Sea Gives Up Its Dead

A Thrilling Detective Story

Elizabeth Burgoyne Corbett

MINT EDITIONS

When the Sea Gives Up Its Dead: A Thrilling Detective Story
was first published in 1894.

This edition published by Mint Editions 2021.

ISBN 9781513299488 | E-ISBN 9781513223926

Published by Mint Editions®

MINT
EDITIONS
minteditionbooks.com

Publishing Director: Jennifer Newens
Design & Production: Rachel Lopez Metzger
Project Manager: Micaela Clark
Typesetting: Westchester Publishing Services

CONTENTS

I

"The Diamond Robbery"

C onfound that upset! I shall be two minutes behind time—I wish I had walked all the way, instead of trusting to the supposed extra speed of a 'bus, when the streets are so slippery that horses cannot keep their feet."

Thus soliloquised Harley Riddell, ruefully, as he hurriedly picked his way through the somewhat aggressive conglomeration of wagons, hansoms, 'buses and fourwheelers, which threatened to still further belate his arrival at the establishment of his employers, Messrs. Stavanger, Stavanger and Co., diamond merchants, of Hatton Garden.

By dint of an extra spurt from the corner of Holborn Viaduct, he managed to be less unpunctual than he had expected; but, somewhat to his surprise, he fancied that the assistants whom he encountered betrayed signs of suppressed excitement, which were not at all in keeping with the usual decorous quietude of Messrs. Stavanger's aristocratic establishment. Still more astonished was he to notice that, whatever the reason for the unusual excitement may have been, it became intensified by his arrival. But there was just a tinge of alarm mingled with his astonishment when he perceived that both the Brothers Stavanger and Mr. Edward Lyon, who was the "Co." in the business, were here before him. As not one of these gentlemen had ever been known to come to business before eleven o'clock in the forenoon, Harley may be excused for thinking it odd that they should all be here on this particular morning before the city clocks had boomed ten, and that, furthermore, they should all stand gazing at him with expressions which suggested suspicion and anathema.

"Nothing wrong, I hope, sirs?" was Harley's impulsive question.

"You are no doubt the best judge of that," said Mr. David Stavanger, who, being a vicar's churchwarden, systematically cultivated a dignified bearing and an impressive mode of speech. "Probably the atrocious injury to which we have been subjected has been exposed to the light of detection sooner than you bargained for. You perceive, Mr. Detective," he continued, turning to a short, but very well-built man of middle age, who was also contemplating our hero with unusual interest, "you perceive the instantaneous working of an evil conscience! No sooner does this ingrate see us here a few moments before our usual time than he jumps to the very natural conclusion that he is at the end of his criminal tether."

"I beg your pardon," interrupted the detective, whose name was John Gay. "Your deductions, Mr. Stavanger, are possibly more decided than correct. We have yet to hear what this gentleman has to say for himself, and you will perhaps let me remind you that it is dangerous to make statements that we perhaps may be unable to prove."

"Gentleman, indeed!" exclaimed Mr. David.

"Yes sir, with your permission, gentleman—until we have proved him otherwise."

"That will be an easy matter," put in Hugh Stavanger, the son of the senior partner. "Everything points to him, and him alone, as the thief."

Harley had not noticed Hugh Stavanger's presence until he thus unpleasantly made it apparent. He had, in fact, been stupefied by the extraordinary words and behaviour of those around him. But at the word "thief" every fibre of his body thrilled with passion, and he strode hastily forward to the side of Hugh Stavanger, exclaiming "Retract that word! or, by Heaven—"

"Ah! he would add violence to his other crimes," said Mr. David, hastily sheltering himself behind Mr. Samuel Stavanger's more portly person. "Take care, Hugh, my boy! There is never any knowing how far these desperadoes will go when they are aroused. Mr. Gay, I insist upon your duty being done at once."

By this time Harley was calm again outwardly, but his calm was as that of the ocean which a deluge of rain is beating into a surface smoothness which the still heaving waters below would fain convert into mountainous breakers.

Thief! Desperado! Was it possible that he was alluded to? He looked at the faces of those around him, and read condemnation in them all. Nay, there was at least one countenance which was impassive, one breast in which a trace of fairplay seemed to linger. He would appeal to the detective for an explanation of this horrible mystery.

"Will you," he began, in a voice whose steadiness and quietness surprised even himself, "will you tell me what is the matter? and why I am glared at as if I were a wild beast?"

"Yes, pray go through the mockery of an explanation," cried Mr. David.

"Sir," replied Mr. Gay, "it is by no means certain that an explanation would be a mockery in this case."

"Why, you yourself said everything pointed to this man's guilt," contended Mr. David.

"Very likely," was the dry reply. "I said that everything seemed to point to your manager's guilt. But I did not say that it proved it. That is another thing, and slightly out of my province."

"And meanwhile," said Harley, "I am still in the dark."

"There has been a robbery of a serious and extensive nature, and you are suspected of being the thief," said the detective, carefully watching the face of the stricken Harley. "It is my duty to arrest you in the name of the law, and I warn you against saying anything that may be construed against you at the trial."

"Since when has this tremendous robbery taken place?" asked Harley. "Everything was secure when I left the premises last night at seven o'clock."

"Who was here when you left?" asked Mr. Lyon, taking part in the conversation for the first time.

"No one, sir. The members of the firm had all left early. Mr. Hugh, to whom I usually hand the keys, being also gone, I locked all the cases up, lighted the gas, padlocked the door, delivered the door-key to the night-watchman, and took the keys of the safes to Mr. David Stavanger's house. I put them into his own hands."

"That is quite true, so far as the delivery of the keys goes," said Mr. David. "What I want to know is this—What have you done with the stones you abstracted before you locked the safes?"

"Excuse me once more," interrupted the detective, "you will have all necessary questions fully answered at the preliminary inquiry. Meanwhile Mr. Harley Riddell must consider himself a prisoner."

"You will permit me to send a message to my brother?"

"Certainly."

One of the shopmen, to whom Harley had always been kind, hurriedly produced a piece of paper and a pencil, and Harley, in whom surprise at his own calmness was still the dominant sensation, quickly wrote as follows:—"Dear Lad, I believe I am under arrest for wholesale robbery. It would be too absurd to protest my innocence to my twin soul. Ascertain where I am taken to, and break the news gently to the dear mother, before it reaches her in someother way. Tell her that the mystery is bound to be cleared up soon. As for Annie—God help her and me, for how can she ally herself to a man who has been under arrest?—Harley."

II

Firm Faith is Not Idle

Harley Riddell was duly charged before a magistrate with having feloniously abstracted gems to the value of four thousand pounds from the premises of Messrs. Stavanger, Stavanger, and Co., diamond merchants. After hearing all the evidence obtainable, the legal luminary thought it his duty to commit the prisoner to the Assizes, and during that time Harley was condemned to undergo the miseries of confinement and mental torture, without being able to do anything to help himself out of the abyss of disgrace into which he had been plunged.

But though he was powerless himself, others were working bravely for him. At first they also worked hopefully, until it became evident that whoever had concocted the plot of which he was the victim, had neglected no precaution against the failure of their plans. Mr. David Stavanger, the senior partner of the firm, deposed that, influenced by the invariable steadiness, industry, and ability of the prisoner, he had been induced to place more trust in him than he had ever placed in any of the subordinates of the firm. He had been eight years in the employment of Messrs. Stavanger, Stavanger, and Co., and had never given the firm any cause to complain of his conduct until now. "In fact," continued Mr. David, "he has so wormed himself into our confidence that it has been a very easy matter for him to steal those jewels, and there is no knowing—"

Considerably to Mr. David's chagrin, however, he was not permitted to continue his remarks, and his evident determination to take accused's guilt for granted was sharply reprimanded. Fellow employees gave similar evidence to that of Mr. David, but were all so evidently convinced of Harley's innocence, that counsel for the prosecution no longer felt quite sure of winning the case, until Mr. Gay produced the most damning evidence that could be forthcoming against a man accused of theft. He had, duly armed with a warrant, searched the belongings of Harley Riddell at his own home, and, inside the lining of the light topcoat that he had worn the day before the occurrence of the robbery, the detective had found three of the missing jewels set as rings, which were identified by Mr. Hugh Stavanger, who had seen them in their cases on the 17th of May.

Asked how, if Harley Riddell was the manager, and consequently of considerable importance in the business, it came to pass that the full extent of the robbery was discovered before the arrival of the latter on the scene, Mr. Hugh Stavanger stated that it was usual for Riddell to see to the safety of everything at the shop and to deliver the keys to the senior partner. At nine in the morning these were fetched by the leading shopman, whose duty it was to see that all was in readiness to receive customers at ten o'clock. As Mr. David Stavanger wished to present his eldest daughter with a birthday gift, Mr. Hugh had volunteered to fetch several articles of jewellery for her to choose from, and had, therefore, contrary to his usual custom, gone to the shop at nine o'clock. He had himself unlocked the safes, and on comparing the contents with the inventory which was with them, had at once seen that a great number of valuable stones were missing, and had telegraphed to the members of the firm to come at once. The detective, who was immediately sent for, could find no evidence that any part of the premises had been feloniously entered, or that the safes had been tampered with.

There was much other evidence, some of it of not too relevant a nature, but all of it conducive to the annihilation of any hope of acquittal for the prisoner. His defence was considered feeble, his guilt indisputable, and he was sentenced to five years' penal servitude.

Five years' penal servitude! Is any pen powerful enough to picture all that it means to a man like Harley Riddell? One day on the summit of bliss, and the next in the abyss of degradation and despair! One day revelling in love and happiness; the next loaded with misery, desperation, and isolation from all his beloved ones! It is terrible for those who are guilty of crime. But for those who are innocent—God help them!

There was a farewell scene between Harley and his mother, who was passionately indignant at the monstrous injustice of which one of her twin sons was the victim. The poor soul, mindful in her misery of Harley's solicitude on her behalf, bravely hid her agonising grief under a show of mingled anger and hopefulness, while for the first time in all her long years of widowhood she felt resigned to the fact that the father of her boys no longer lived to witness the disgrace that had fallen upon his name. What though the disgrace was unmerited! It was none the less bitter, and Harley, who knew his mother's indomitable nature, felt cheered and hopeful in his turn when he heard her vow to use every means, whether they were evidently possible or apparently impossible, to vindicate his character, and bring the guilt of the robbery home to the real perpetrators. Hilton Riddell, his twin brother, cheered him much, too, by his faith in the chances of a speedy unravelment of the plot of which he was evidently the victim.

There was also another with whom a parting interview was permitted, although Harley would almost have preferred to be spared the anguish of mind which it cost him. For the presence of winsome Annie Cory, who was to have been his bride ere long, only brought the more vividly to his mind the picture of all that cruel fate had bereft him of.

She, like the true girl she was, vowed to wait for his release, and to wed none but him. He, being sensitive and refined, vowed just as positively that nothing but the most incontrovertible proofs of his innocence would ever permit him to take advantage of her love.

Mr. Cory was very magnanimous, and he had cordially approved of the engagement of his only child to a man whose combined resources only amounted to £400 a year. For was not he himself wealthy enough to provide very handsomely for his daughter, and were not the various qualities of Harley Riddell far beyond riches alone?

Still, although he liked the young fellow, and would, under happier conditions, have gladly welcomed him as a son-in-law, he fully endorsed Harley's protestations to the effect that only as a man who could stand before the world unshamed would he ever permit a woman to share his life. For he would not like his daughter to marry an ex-convict, whom folks would look askance at, even though the ex-convict's friends were all convinced of his innocence and of the injustice of his punishment.

But he deemed it wise to offer no violent opposition to Annie's determination to be true to the man she loved. He trusted to time to weaken her love, and show her the folly of allying herself to poverty and disgrace. Meanwhile, as he really liked Harley, and fully believed in his innocence, he meant to do all in his power to promote a certain plan which Hilton had confided to him, whereby it was hoped to divert the weight of punishment on to the shoulders that deserved it.

The interview had proved trying to Annie as well as to Harley, and Mr. Cory was very thankful when he arrived at his own house with his daughter, who certainly looked as if she had borne as much as she could.

"Margaret," he said to his sister, who had been his housekeeper ever since his wife died, eight years before the opening of our story, "I believe the child is dead beat, and I don't feel too clever myself. Have you anything in the way of a pick-me-up ready?"

"You shall have some hot milk, with a touch of brandy in it, in a few minutes. That will do you both good, and serve to put you off until dinner is ready, which will be another half hour yet. How did the child bear it?"

"Very bravely. Vowed eternal fidelity, and all that sort of thing. But Riddell is too much of a man to take her at her word, and swears to be nobody's husband until he is proved innocent. And quite right, too. In fact, I hope Annie will get over her infatuation in any case, for I have no fancy for being pointed at as the father-in-law of a man who has been in gaol. You see, although we never for a moment believe that the poor lad had anything to do with the robbery, and are sure that he is the victim of a vile plot, it will be difficult to get the world to think as we do, and, to tell the truth, it's a deucedly nasty business all round."

While Mr. Cory had been speaking, Annie had gone up to her own room, and Miss Cory had rung her bell in order to give some directions to a servant before she followed her niece upstairs.

"Williamson," she said, "bring two glasses of hot milk here as quickly as possible."

She delivered herself of this order very quietly. But no sooner was the servant's back turned than she emptied the vials of her wrath on to her brother's devoted head.

"John Cory," she said, drawing her really majestic figure up to its full height, and speaking with a solemn deliberation which she only affected on serious occasions. "I'm ashamed of you! I never expected to see the day when my father's son would deliberately contemplate the desertion and permanent abandonment of a man whose sole sin is his betrayal by some villain who has cunningly contrived to divert suspicion from himself to an innocent man. John Cory, if I could believe that you would do this vile thing, I would leave your roof forever."

"But, my dear girl—"

"Don't 'my dear girl' me! You never do it except when you want to talk me over, and at fifty-six I'm too old to swallow gross flattery. Just tell me this—Do you mean to turn your back on young Riddell now that he is powerless to help himself, or do you mean to act like a man?"

"Of course, I mean to do all I can for him."

"I knew you did. All the same, the bare thought that you could dream of revoking what you promised just before the poor lad's calamity overtook him, made me feel as if I could shake you. Oh, here's your milk. Just put your brandy in yourself and drink it, while I go upstairs to Annie. Williamson, see that we have dinner punctually."

Williamson, having acknowledged her mistress's order with due deference, hurried away to expedite matters in the lower regions, and Miss Margaret Cory lost no more time in visiting her niece, whom she found sobbing as though her heart was breaking. At this sight, even Miss Margaret, stolid though she usually was, found herself considerably upset. She made a faint attempt to dissuade Annie from crying, but was convinced that her efforts were woefully inadequate, and eventually administered the truest consolation by breaking down herself and mingling her tears with those of the girl whom she loved more than any other being on earth.

"There, auntie, I won't be so foolish again," said Annie at last. "But I could not help myself when I thought of all the horrors poor Harley is doomed to endure."

"And no wonder, my dear. But, please God, we'll put an end to his misery by freeing him before long."

"But how can that be? Have you forgotten that he is sentenced to five years' imprisonment?"

"No, I have not forgotten. Neither have I forgotten a speech that his brother Hilton uttered last night. He said:—'Heaven helping me, I will leave no stone unturned to run the author of all this misery to earth. He may be very cunning, but I defy him to elude my watchfulness, when once I have set eyes upon him. The mystery is not so great as it perhaps seems to some. The onus of criminality rests between very few people, and I have good reasons for believing that my suspicions are centring themselves round the right man. It is but a question of time, for, if there is a God in Heaven, the guilty coward who really stole those diamonds shall be brought to justice!' Annie, when I heard the fervour with which those words were uttered, and marked the deliberate determination of Hilton Riddell's mien, I shared his confidence in the future, and resolved to afford him every facility for achieving his purpose. He will need money, for without money very little can be done. For your sake, my darling, I will give all I can to prove your lover's innocence."

"How good you are, auntie!" cried the girl, kissing her relative affectionately. "You always make me feel better. This time, besides comforting me, you have made me a little bit ashamed of myself. Henceforth I will work, instead of giving way to useless repining. If there is any part I can take in the unravelment of this mystery, I will show myself a ready and capable helper."

"That's right, dear girl. The police started with the conviction that Harley Riddell was guilty, and hunted up no end of facts to prove themselves in the right. We will start with equally positive convictions in the other direction, and it will be odds if our labour of love does not bear the fruit we desire."

"Oh, auntie! I am all anxiety to begin! Do let me run down and tell the dad all about it."

"Not so fast, my dear. If Mrs. Riddell, who has been terribly prostrated by this blow, is able to bear being left an hour or two this evening, her son will call here, by appointment with me, to consult as to what will be the best plans for us to adopt."

"You dear old thing! You have been actually working already!"

"Certainly. The sooner we begin operating, the better chance we have of being successful, and the sooner we may hope to see Harley justified and at liberty. In fact, you need not be surprised if Hilton Riddell has already made considerable progress. And now, dear, you must make yourself a little presentable, and I expect you to partake of a substantial meal, even as I mean to do, for we must make ourselves strong if we mean to do anything useful."

The result of Miss Margaret's tact and management was that Annie was not nearly so downcast that evening as her father had feared she would be, and when Hilton Riddell made his appearance at eight o'clock, he found every member of the Cory family ready and willing to second all his endeavours on Harley's behalf.

"And how did you leave your mother?" asked Miss Margaret.

"Stronger and better than I could have believed possible," was the reply. "She is brave and hopeful, and firmly believes that I shall succeed in tracing the real delinquent. One thing troubles me a good deal about my mother. It may be necessary for me to travel, or someother contingency may arise which will render it impossible to be with her much, and I fear that, if left to herself, she may succumb to her troubles."

"She shall not be left to herself," cried Miss Margaret, emphasising her remarks by a vigorous shake of the handsome lace lappets which adorned her cap. "She must come and live here while you are away. That is just what you would have proposed yourself, isn't it, John?"

"Certainly, just the very thing," echoed John, warmly. "Sorry you got the suggestion out before I did, though. And now, Mr. Riddell, about your means and employment. Don't think me impertinent or intrusive, but—"

"Pray don't apologise," said Hilton, hastily. "I will, as you so kindly take such an interest in us, explain exactly how we stand. My mother, who is an officer's widow, has a life pension, which the vicissitudes in the career of Harley or myself cannot touch. My employers, Messrs. Treadonem and Co., have magnanimously given me my liberty, and have not been afraid to mention their true reason for discarding the services of the brother of a convict. My time, therefore, is my own, to use as I please. Needless to say, it will be used in my brother's service. Fortunately, I have a couple of hundred pounds saved, and Harley, during the last six years, has saved a few hundreds also. He has some inkling of my intended course of procedure, and has arranged for me to draw his money, if I require it. But I hope to run my quarry to earth without encroaching upon Harley's savings, for it will go hard with him at first, especially if he has no money to fall back upon."

"His money shall not be touched," put in Mr. Cory in a very decided tone. "I have a nice sum available for unexpected contingencies like the present."

"And so have I," answered Miss Margaret.

"You are very kind; I hardly know how to thank you," said Hilton, very much moved.

"And how can I help?" inquired Annie, piteously. "I have no money of my own, but I am anxious to do some real work, and I am sure you would find me clever and capable."

"I should only be too glad of your help," said Hilton, with animation in his mien and entreaty in his voice, "but the only way in which you can help seems too preposterous to suggest to you."

"Out with it, man," cried Mr. Cory; "if it is something that cannot be undertaken, no harm will be done."

"Then here you are, sir. It is necessary that I should gain a little insight into the doings of the family of Mr. David Stavanger, for I am convinced that either he or his son knows where the still missing diamonds could be found. There is an advertisement in today's paper for a holiday governess to the youngest Miss Stavanger, a girl of twelve. Tomorrow morning I intended going to the office of Messrs. Bell and White, private inquiry agents, to ask them to send their principal lady detective, Miss Dora Bell, to try for the appointment, as a governess has many means of gaining information concerning what is going on in a household. Now, if you—"

"Not another word, I will turn detective, and beard these lions in their own den," was Annie's exclamation.

"But how about references? Besides, they would know your name, perhaps," objected Mr. Cory.

"You dear innocent," remarked Miss Margaret, with the calmness born of superior wisdom; "when one takes up detective work, one has not to be too squeamish about ways and means, and you may trust us to devise some scheme to circumvent these villains. If Annie can't get the post, I'll try to make myself look more youthful, and make a bid for the appointment."

Somehow, any lurking objections which Mr. Cory might have had were all overcome, and when Hilton went home that night, many arrangements for the future had been made. Subject to Mrs. Riddell's own consent, it had been decided that it would be best for her to live with Miss Margaret for a while. Mr. Cory, very much to his own surprise, found himself enrolled as an amateur detective, liable to be called upon for active service at anytime. Annie, instead of moping at home and giving way to melancholy, was bent upon yielding efficient help as a lady detective, and Hilton meant to be guided by the exigencies of the moment.

The avowed end and aim of all these good people was to bring the man who was responsible for Harley Riddell's imprisonment to justice.

The progress of our story will show how they went about their new employment, and what were the results of their endeavours as amateur detectives.

III

"Miss Annie Cory is Confidential"

A few days after the events narrated in the last chapter, Miss Margaret Cory was reading aloud from some manuscript which she had just received by post. Her audience was small, being composed of two individuals with whom we are already acquainted—to wit, her brother, Mr. Cory, and Hilton Riddell, who both listened to her with curious interest.

You and I too, dear readers, will take the liberty of hearing what Miss Cory had to say.

"My darling Auntie," she read, "I am now fairly installed here, but, would you believe it? there are signs already that it will be unnecessary for me to remain here very long. I shall, however, do my utmost to retard my exit until I have learned all I want to know. Short as my time here has been, it has already revealed much to me. Perhaps I had better begin my story at the beginning, and then you can form your own opinion. I must also be as lucid and explicit as possible, since upon what I learn and describe Hilton Riddell's actions in the near future are dependent.

"On presenting myself here yesterday morning, according to arrangement, I was admitted by a middle-aged servant, who regarded me with what I considered pure effrontery.

"'I wish to see Mrs. Stavanger,' I said.

"'Very likely,' was the woman's answer. 'But you may prepare yourself for a long wait first.'

"'Why? Is she not in?'

"'Oh yes, she's in. But she thinks people wouldn't believe her to be a swell if she didn't keep folks waiting a good bit.'

"'Perhaps you will be good enough to tell her that I am here.'

"'I suppose you are the new governess?'

"'I am.'

"'Oh well, you won't be here long, if you've no more patience than the others. But come inside; you can wait in the hall.'

"Saying this, the extraordinary specimen of a servant permitted me to cross the threshold. The cabman had become impatient, and began to bring my bit of luggage in at once. It was quite ten minutes before the woman, who, I learned afterwards, is called Wear, made her reappearance, and requested me to follow her to the drawing-room. By this time the cabman had been paid and had gone away.

"Still smarting under the peculiar treatment of the servant, it was with some trepidation that I approached the mistress. She was sitting in an easy chair, and did not rise to greet me, as I naturally expected she would do. From this trifling circumstance I instantly deduced the opinion that Mrs. Stavanger was totally devoid of those finer instincts which go to make up the being described by the term 'lady.' Subsequent observations have confirmed me in this opinion. Personal beauty of a strong, showy type, must at one time have been Mrs. Stavanger's to a great degree. She would be handsome yet, but for the expression of mingled ill-temper and arrogance which perpetually disfigures her features. She is, I think, a woman who has, by means of her good looks, secured a husband whose position in life is much higher than hers had been, and she is one of those people of whom it is expressively said that 'they cannot carry corn'—in other words she is a 'beggar on horseback.'

"She treated me with scant courtesy, even as her waiting maid had led me to expect. She apparently imagines that a woman who is compelled to earn her living in any shape or form is no longer deserving of respect or civility. Hers is a belief which, unfortunately, has many followers, but which troubles me very little, and would trouble me just as little were I really the poor governess I seem to be, for I do not hold the opinion of unreasonable people to be important enough to worry about. By the time this interview was over, I had been given to understand that my duties would be slightly more onerous than I had anticipated when being engaged by Mr. Stavanger, who had spoken of his wife being too nervous to interview strangers, and of his twelve-year-old daughter as a child who required very little discipline.

"The latter is a very bright girl, but she is fearfully spoiled by alternate over-indulgence and fault-finding. She has led her former governess a pretty dance, by all accounts, and coolly told me that she always did as she liked, and that it was no use telling tales of her, as her mother never believed them, but invariably punished the governess instead of the refractory pupil.

"'It's no use your setting me any lessons,' she remarked yesterday afternoon. 'I shall only work when I like, just as I have always done.'

"'Very well,' I replied coolly, 'we'll be idle together. It's no use killing oneself to keep oneself, is it?'

"You would have been highly amused if you had seen Miss Fanny Stavanger's stare of surprise. She is evidently not used to being humoured.

"'I don't know,' was her dubious answer to my query. 'If you take your wages you ought to try to earn them. That is what mamma always tells the other servants.'

"This wasn't a palatable speech to hear. But the stake for which I am playing is too big to allow me to be daunted by trifles, so I merely told the girl it rested entirely with her whether I accepted my 'wages' from her parents or not, and that if she refused to learn her lessons there would be no alternative for me but to refuse.

"'Perhaps,' I added, 'you have been harassed over your lessons and have not been permitted to learn in your own way. If you like we will alter all that. You shall study when you please, and give over the minute you are tired.'

"'Well, I call you really jolly,' was Miss Fanny's rejoinder. 'Maybe you think me a fool, but if you'll help me nicely, you'll see what a lot I can really do.'

"The little rebel was conquered. This morning she was quite eager to begin studying with me, and I foresee little trouble with her in future. Already she begins to be confidential with me, and has told me something that will prove valuable. I am, I suppose, not yet quite inured to my duties as detective, for I felt downright mean when listening to Fanny, until a picture of my poor, innocent Harley rose before my mental vision, and my heart hardened against the wicked people who have ruined him.

"There are several members of this household who would prove interesting to a student of human nature. Mr. Stavanger is purse-proud, ostentatiously religious, hard and uncharitable in his judgment of others; fond of show, and yet mean in trifles. It needs no very keen observer to discover that much.

"Of Mrs. Stavanger you will already have formed your opinion. The eldest daughter is a conglomeration of both parents, with some of their defects slightly accentuated. The son I need not describe to you, you saw him at the trial. But Fanny has told me that of late he has been very unsteady, and that he and his father have quarrelled a good deal. My pupil has also much to say about Wear, the parlour maid.

"'I never saw anybody change so,' observed the child. 'Wear used to be so respectful, until those nasty thieves got into the shop, and nearly ruined papa and his partners. Since then she is impertinent all day long, and says such queer things. I can't imagine why she isn't packed off about her business. But when Ada told her the other day that she would put up with her impudence no longer, Wear just laughed in her face, and said that it would take a cleverer body than Ada to turn her out of this house now.'

"I made no comments to Fanny on this information. But I feel sure of one thing. Wear has become possessed of some power over the Stavangers, of which she is making a very injudicious use, since it would pay her in the end much better to keep a civil tongue in her head, and merely to insist upon more liberal wages, instead of showing others that there is ground for suspicion. When once the source of her sudden accession of power over the Stavangers is discovered that power will irrevocably leave her. Coupling Fanny's remarks about 'those nasty thieves' with our own previously-formed opinion respecting the actual culprit in whose place Harley has been condemned and Wear's peculiar behaviour, the inference that we are on the right track is obvious. With God's help, we shall yet be able to rescue Harley from his horrible fate. I wonder if you will think me wicked when I confess that I long for the time when his betrayers will be suffering the agony that has been meted out to him. Tell Hilton to hold himself in readiness for action at any moment, for I am sure that I am on the eve of further discoveries."

Three days later another budget from Annie was being discussed in Mr. Cory's drawing-room. This time Miss Cory had an additional listener. Mrs. Riddell had been persuaded to take up her abode here for an indefinite period. Her house had been let furnished until such time as she was likely to require it again. Hilton was also visiting here at present, and was ready to do anything or go anywhere to help to prove his brother's innocence. The fact that his mother was in such good hands, instead of being left to mope and grieve in childless loneliness, heartened him considerably for the work which he was convinced lay before him.

"Since writing to you last," read Miss Cory, "I have made a wonderful discovery. I am quite sure that Hugh Stavanger, whose evidence was the principal means of ensuring Harley's condemnation, is the thief we are in search of. Last night at twelve o'clock, when all the household was supposed to be asleep, Mr. Stavanger was fuming in the dining-room at the belated return home of his hopeful son, who, I have gathered, has got into the habit of staying out late at night. At eleven o'clock I had heard the hall door open, and someone ran upstairs to Hugh Stavanger's room, shutting the bedroom door behind him. The servants, who had not seen the entrance of Mr. Hugh, but had heard the noisy run up to his room, concluded that it was he who had come in. Everybody else being at home, they locked and barred the doors for the night, and then went to bed. But I, who had resolved to let nothing escape my notice, if it could be helped, knew that a little pantomime was being enacted for the benefit of the unsuspicious servants, for it was Mr. Stavanger who had come noiselessly downstairs, and had imitated his son's manner of entering the house and going upstairs. The latter was still away from home.

"From this behaviour I drew certain deductions. Mr. Stavanger wanted to speak privately to his son; he did not want the servants to witness the time of Hugh's arrival, nor the condition in which he arrived; and the matter about which he desired to speak must be of great importance, since it required to be discussed unseasonably.

"I determined to be present at the interview.

"To do this, prompt action on my part was necessary, as I must be on the scene before either of the principal actors. There are three servants in the house. Wear was the last of these to go to bed, and the moment she had passed the landing on to which my room door opened, I slipped downstairs, and passed quietly into the dining room, without being heard by anyone. Then I hid myself behind the window draperies, and awaited events.

"I had not long to wait. Scarcely two minutes had elapsed ere Mr. Stavanger, slipperless and cautious, came creeping into the room. Perhaps it was because he was nervous that he found it necessary to help himself to a big drink of brandy. Having disposed of this, he stepped softly into the hall, and, an instant later, I heard him carefully unfastening the front door. I was very glad that he did not return to the dining room immediately, as this enabled me to change my position into a more comfortable one. I sat down on the floor, leaned my back against one of the window frames, and readjusted the curtains.

"If there was to be an interview between father and son, I might expect them in this room, for they were not likely to be so indiscreet as to carry on a conversation in the hall. Nor was I mistaken. In about a quarter of an hour I heard someone ascend the front steps, and Mr. Stavanger, who had been waiting in the hall until then, opened the door before his son had time either to ring the bell or to insert a latch key.

"'Keep yourself quiet,' I heard him say in a low tone, 'and go into the dining room. Make no noise, for your liberty is in danger.'

ELIZABETH BURGOYNE CORBETT

"Do you believe that, in cases of emergency, some of our faculties are strengthened to an enormous extent? I think that this must be so, and that I, for one, have been the subject of this phenomenon. Otherwise, how shall I account for being able to hear Mr. Stavanger's words so distinctly? No doubt, the midnight quiet of the house and neighbourhood had something to do with it. Still, I shall always think that Providence thus showed its approval of my endeavours to save Harley Riddell from an unjust fate.

"Hugh's answer to his father's injunction was an exclamation of which I did not catch the import. But he was evidently sufficiently impressed by his manner to be obedient for once. I heard the door quietly fastened again, and then the two men came into the room in which I was playing the eavesdropper. Mr. Stavanger, after turning up the gas, which he had previously lighted, seated himself, and requested his son to do the same.

"'Now then,' observed the latter, 'I would like to know what all this mystery is about, and what you mean by insinuating that my liberty is in danger.'

"'Have you no idea?' questioned Mr. Stavanger.

"'Not the slightest.'

"'Think again.'

"'Why the deuce don't you out with it? It isn't likely that I know just what you are driving at, and if I did, I am not fool enough to take the initiative.'

"'Well I will tell you. I have all along suspected that you yourself were the thief for whom Riddell has been made the scapegoat. Perhaps it will be as well for me to tell you that I have from the first been sure of it. This was what made me so anxious to secure Riddell's conviction. I hoped thereby to save our own name from disgrace. But my efforts are likely to prove futile, because, besides being a thief, a perjurer, and a scoundrel, you are proving yourself a fool. You have been spending and gambling recklessly of late, and people are talking about the amount of money you are getting through. The gossip about you has come to Mr. Lyon's ears, and today I endured the greatest humiliation of my life, for I was told to my face that I had deliberately sent an innocent man to gaol, knowing the while that my son was guilty. It was in vain that I denied this. Mr. Lyon vows that he has proofs of your guilt, and he has given me his positive orders to refund the value of the theft and to endorse some story which he is going to trump up to show that no theft has been committed, or take the consequences.'

"'Meaning that he would make me change places with Riddell! Good God! what shall I do? I can't give up the diamonds!'

"'But you must give them up! Do you think I will allow you to ruin us all? And simply because you want money to squander in drinking and gambling hells? Tell me what you have done with your booty.'

"'It's all gone. I realised the diamonds for a quarter their value, and paid my creditors with it.'

"'What! you were heavily in debt?'

"'Yes. I owed hundreds, and the money melted like wax.'

"'What have you left?'

"'About fifty pounds.'

"'It's a lie! You cannot have gone through the worth of all you took.'

"'I tell you I have.'

"'I wonder what I have done that I should be cursed by a son like you! I won't ruin myself to buy your freedom. You shall go to gaol like the dog you are.'

"'And what about the mater and the girls? If you won't do it for me, you will perhaps wish you had done it for their sakes.'

"'Ah, you have me there! You are not worth stretching out a saving hand to. But it would be hard to make them suffer for you.'

"'Yes, I knew I should bring you to reason. What do you intend to do in the matter?'

"'Do you think your equal for shamelessness could be found anywhere?'

"'Suppose you stick to business. What is going to be done?'

"'Mr. Lyon sails for America tomorrow on very important business, as you already know. He will not remain there above a week. In three weeks, therefore, we may expect him back. Before that time arrives two things must be done. I must place to the credit of Mr. Lyon and your uncle Samuel an equivalent for their share of the stolen property. And you must have left the country before then, for he has forbidden your entering the shop again, and will not pledge himself not to denounce you if he sees you.'

"'But this is no reason why I should leave England?'

"'There is another reason.'

"'What is that?'

"'Wear knows your secret. She saw the box of diamonds in your room on the day of the robbery. At first she did not think about it, but, after hearing of the robbery she put two and two together, and concluded that the fine things that were missing were the same which her prying eyes had seen hidden in the corner of one of your drawers. I can't imagine how a man in your position could be fool enough to leave his drawers unlocked. Anyhow, Wear fathomed your secret, and tried to find the things again, but they were gone. Then she came to me, and threatened exposure unless I gave her fifty pounds to hold her tongue. This I did, hoping to hear no more of the matter from her. But she is a woman of such little sense that she is likely to ruin everything. Not content with demanding more money from time to time, she is vilely impertinent to us all, and behaves so very much like a person who holds us under her thumb, that I shall find it necessary to make some provision for her further away. But first, you must clear out of the country, for your conduct is such as to awaken too much suspicion.'

"'Does the mater know all?'

"'No. She knows that Wear holds you in her power somehow, but doesn't know the actual facts. I was obliged to get up a plausible yarn as wide of the real truth as I could, in order to induce her to keep Wear on, now that she is so impertinent, until I could get rid of her diplomatically.'

"'And when must I go?'

"'Tomorrow night, at nine o'clock, a certain Captain Cochrane will call to escort you to his ship. You must have everything in readiness to leave with him. But you will not be able to take any luggage with you, as Wear must not know you are going away.'

"'Send Wear out of the way somewhere. Pack her off to the Crystal Palace for the day.'

"'It won't do. Our servants are not used to treats, and Wear would suspect something in a minute. Besides, I don't want anybody except Captain Cochrane to know that I am cognisant of your departure. It may save a good deal of awkwardness for me in future.'

"This conversation, as you may easily believe, was listened to by me with the greatest eagerness, and I was desperately afraid of missing a word. Here was full proof to me, of Harley's innocence. But my knowledge was, I knew, useless as evidence, since I had no witness but myself to bring forward. True, there is Wear. But she may be bought over by the other side. And at present our task must be the frustration of Hugh Stavanger's attempt to escape with the diamonds. For, in spite of his assertion to the contrary, I believe him to be still in possession of the greater part of the stolen property. If he goes away with Captain Cochrane, he will contrive to take his booty on board with him.

"There is one thing that makes my discoveries incomplete. Otherwise I would have come home to tell you all this, never to return here, instead of sitting up all night to write this. The name of the ship in which Hugh Stavanger is to sail did not transpire, so Hilton will not be able to do anything to help until tomorrow night. He must then watch for the arrival of this captain, and be prepared to follow him and his intended companion wherever they may go. It may be necessary to try to obtain a passage with them. Is there any office on board a ship that Hilton can take?

"Tomorrow night, if I see an opportunity of hearing what these bad people have to say to each other, I will try to gain some additional information, for use in case Hilton fails to get on board with them, or to intercept Hugh Stavanger's attempt to escape. Perhaps I may learn something more during the day. But this meeting is too early for me to have any prospect of hiding unobserved, for the rest of the household will all be up and stirring. Even if I could secrete myself again, I might not be able to escape detection and reach my own room unobserved, as I have been able to do this last night.

"The fact is, I feel somewhat unnerved, and am afraid of betraying myself. In a few hours I must go through the farce of teaching Fanny, although I feel dead tired already. I shall not need to feign a headache. Still, if needs were, I could spend many a night in the work of love upon which I have entered, and the day will wear away as others do. Then as soon as I feel that my further presence here is useless, I will try to slip out unobserved and exchange experiences with Hilton, if there is time before the two men leave the house. As you know, I brought very little luggage with me, and I will put on as many clothes as possible, leaving the few things I cannot use. They are not marked, and I could not be traced through them, especially as I am dyed and painted to look like somebody else for awhile."

This was all. Annie left off abruptly. Possibly she had feared interruption; or had had only time enough to catch the early morning post. Anyhow, she had done her part of the investigations well, and had sent a very comprehensive report.

"Isn't she a splendid girl?" said Miss Cory, with enthusiasm.

"She is just wonderful," answered Hilton. "No wonder my brother loves her so. I wish the world held more like her."

"There are heaps of brave and noble girls, my boy, if you only knew where to look for them. I wish my poor child was nicely out of that nest of scoundrels."

To which remark of Mr. Cory's Mrs. Riddell, wiping first her eyes and then her spectacles, gave answer—"Mr. Cory, that girl is too plucky and sensible to get into trouble through being indiscreet. And as nothing else is likely to betray her identity, we may rest assured that she will get away all right. She will have no great distance to travel, but of course, someone must be on the lookout for her."

"I will go with Hilton," said Mr. Cory; "and we will be within watching distance of Mr. Stavanger's house before half-past eight. Then, everything being arranged that requires to be arranged beforehand, Hilton will follow the two men, and find out what ship they are bound for, while I wait for Annie, and bring her home with me."

"Her suggestion that, if Hugh Stavanger gets to sea before the diamonds can be found, as proof of what she says, I should try to embark on board the same ship, with the object of recovering the things, or indicating their whereabouts to the authorities, is a good one. But I have no experience of sea-life, beyond an occasional excursion for an hour or two from a sea-side holiday resort. And I have not the slightest idea of anything I could do to excuse my presence on board a ship of any sort. The sailors work above, and the firemen below. But even if I knew their duties, and could get a job on board, my chances of finding the diamonds would be small. But I would take care to keep my man in sight after he left the ship, and it will take him all his time to baffle me then."

So said Hilton, and this time it was Miss Cory who made the suggestions which were ultimately followed.

"You couldn't go on board directly after the captain to ask for work. The time would be so unseasonable as to cause suspicion. But you might perhaps ascertain casually whether the ship is leaving at once or not. If it is, then you will have to risk trying to get on board, in spite of the lateness of the hour. If not, wait till morning, but keep watch lest there should be an attempt to slip away earlier than the time mentioned to you. You have several hours yet before you, and you have more than one disguise ready. Use one of these, and pack the others in your box for use in emergencies. Go boldly on board, and offer to pay for your passage. Comport yourself as one who has plenty of money, but who has some reason for preferring to sail in a vessel that is not known as a passenger ship. The captain will at once jump to the conclusion that you are in some trouble, and you must humour his fancy. Hint something about a breach of promise action, and he will think you quite a hero."

The last sentence was uttered with a scornful accent which plainly indicated Miss Cory's opinion of man's peculiar notions of what is honourable in his dealings with the other sex. But her suggestion "caught on," and formed the basis of the tale with which Hilton Riddell was to hide his real motive in attempting to obtain a passage with Captain Cochrane. There was of course the possibility that his application would be refused. In this case, he would proceed by the quickest route to whichever place the merchant ship was bound for, and would be on the spot, ready to meet the diamond thief, and to do his best to convict him of the possession of some of the stolen property.

When, at the time agreed upon, Mr. Cory and Hilton Riddell set off on their mission of love and vengeance, every detail of their plans had been arranged, Hilton, not sure when or under what circumstances he would see his mother again, had bidden her a fond goodbye, and had left her praying for God's help in the enterprise which she hoped would restore her banished son to her.

Meanwhile the Stavangers, father and son, were also maturing their plans, feeling pretty confident now of success, and little dreaming that the avenger was already on their track.

IV

A Suspicious Death

Nearly opposite the residence of Mr. Stavanger there was an untenanted house. The front area was well planted with trees and shrubs, which afforded capital shelter to two men who had loitered there for sometime. The men were known to us, being none other than Mr. Cory and Hilton Riddell. They were getting somewhat fidgety lest a mistake had been made somewhere. For it was long past the time appointed for Hugh Stavanger's departure with Captain Cochrane, and yet they had seen neither the one nor the other, although the house had been strictly watched for two hours.

"He can't have eluded us by going away earlier than the time named?" said Hilton, anxiously.

"Oh no," was the confident reply. "Annie would have been sure to let us know somehow or other."

"Unless she is suspected, and is prevented from doing anything further just now."

"That is possible. But I doubt it, for she would have no need or opportunity to watch Mr. Stavanger in any suspicious way during the day. And even if she had found it desirable to do so, and had been detected, what could these people do to her? They could not say: You shall not go out, because we have been stealing, and don't want to be caught. As for locking her up in her room, that would be hardly practicable. No, since she has not come out to us I fancy that events are still multiplying indoors, and that we shall hear all about it soon. Ah—there is somebody coming out! It is Annie, I expect."

"No; it is a woman, but it is not Miss Cory."

"It is a servant, and on an urgent message, for she is actually running."

"Hush! she might hear us. Now she has passed us. Shall I follow her, do you think?"

"No, no, stay here. Look how the lights are flashing about those upper rooms. The whole house seems to be in an uproar—and now I can hear a woman screaming. Good God! they are murdering Annie."

As he almost shouted this, in his sudden alarm, Mr. Cory, followed by Hilton, rushed across the road and up the steps leading to Mr. Stavanger's house. Someone was evidently expected, for the door was opened as soon as they reached it, and a young girl, the housemaid probably, stood before them with clasped hands and streaming eyes.

"Oh, sir, are you the doctor?" she exclaimed. "It's just awful! Wear has been taken ill all of a sudden, and she is rolling on the floor and screaming dreadful, with the agony she's in. The missis is too frightened to be beside her. But the governess is with her, and oh dear, doctor, do be quick!"

"I'm not the doctor," answered Mr. Cory quickly, "but I'll fetch one directly. I was passing and heard the screams. Come along."

A moment later both men were hastening for a certain Doctor Mayne, whom they knew. He lived not far away, and from him they hoped to be able to hear a few after-details of the case. Fortunately he was at home, and set off at once. The doctor whom the servant had gone to seek had not been in when she arrived at his house, so Doctor Mayne was admitted to the patient at once. But the moment he looked at her he judged her case to be hopeless.

Nor was he mistaken. Poor Wear was, as the housemaid had said, in mortal agony. An hour later she was dead. Annie, though she was tired and heartsick, was with her to the last, rendering what help she could, and wondering all the while if this terrible event could be the accident it was supposed to be. For the woman's death at this juncture, with Hugh Stavanger's secret still unbetrayed by her, was so strangely opportune an occurrence that less suspicious natures than Annie's might easily suspect some of the Stavangers to have had a hand in it.

Wear was known to be rather fond of an occasional drink of Hollands. On her box in her room was found a gin bottle, from which she had evidently been drinking. But the bottle contained no gin, but a deadly poison sometimes used for disinfecting purposes. How this happened to be in an unlabelled bottle, and how Wear happened to mistake it for gin, are mysteries which have never been elucidated, and never will be now. The dead woman can reveal neither of these secrets, nor that other one which was so important to the people in whose house she died.

It was about eleven o'clock when this event occurred.

Meanwhile our two watchers were in a great state of anxiety and suspense, which was not lessened when Doctor Mayne, surprised to see them there still when he left the house, told them that all was over.

"Sometime, Doctor Mayne, I will explain everything to you. At present my great anxiety is about my daughter."

"Why, is she ill?"

"No, she is in that house. The woman who had just died an awful death knew a secret likely to cost young Stavanger his liberty and to liberate young Riddell, and the Stavangers were aware that she had them in her power. My daughter is there. She also knows their secret. Her life is no safer than Wear's was. She shall stay no longer, lest she also be poisoned."

"You are saying terrible things, Mr. Cory," said the doctor, "but your excitement must prove your excuse. The unfortunate woman certainly died from poison. But there is nothing in the event to lead to the supposition that anyone but herself was to blame for the accident. In any case, it is of a kind to which your daughter could hardly fall a victim. Even if Wear had been deliberately poisoned—and I do not for a moment think that is so—a repetition of the same kind of tragedy would not be ventured upon by even the most reckless criminals. The young lady whom I take to be your daughter looked so ill and upset that I advised her to go to bed at once, and I know that she agreed to follow my advice."

"Where is Mr. Stavanger?"

"I do not know. There are no men in the house, I think, at present, and the women are all considerably cut up by tonight's scene. And now, as I have had several broken nights lately, and am very tired, I will say goodbye. Tomorrow I will talk things over."

"Now, what do you think it behoves us to do?" asked Hilton, who was as greatly perplexed and alarmed as Mr. Cory was. "I cannot understand how it happens that the Stavangers, senior and junior, and this Captain Cochrane, of whom Annie spoke, have not turned up."

"I have it," said Mr. Cory, after some deliberation. "There has been some alteration of plans. We left home perhaps earlier than Annie expected, and there may even now be a message waiting for us. But here comes a woman. See how she loiters. One would think she was as much interested in this house as we are."

"Why, so she is! It is Miss Cory, I am sure."

And so it proved. It was Miss Cory indeed, looking for her brother and friend.

"Whatever brings you here, Margaret?" asked Mr. Cory, in considerable surprise.

"Come here and you shall know," she answered. "You can do nothing more here, and I have much to tell you. Annie is not coming out tonight. She is all right. Now listen."

And as the trio walked homewards, Miss Cory gave them the following particulars:

"You had not been gone many minutes," she said, "when a letter from Annie arrived, saying that she would come home tomorrow, as her work would then, she thought, be quite done. She also said that Mrs. Stavanger had received a telegraphic message during the morning. It was addressed to her husband, but she had opened it, as was her usual custom with messages which came to the house. It simply said 'Can't come. Bring H. S. at 8.30 to Millwall Dock. Sail tomorrow.' Annie understood the message, which Mrs. Stavanger indiscreetly read aloud. To the mistress of the house it was not so intelligible. But she comprehended that it might be important, and sent the boy who does odd jobs about the house during the day to the shop with it. It seems to me that it would take a very clever individual to throw dust into Annie's eyes. 'I am not sure,' she writes, 'that it is safe to neglect watching the house, and yet Hilton at least should try to keep Hugh Stavanger in sight. What we want to prove is that he has the diamonds. It is no use, as we know, to attempt to have him arrested until we have proof in our possession that will convict him. Of course we know that he is guilty, and certain other people know it also. But we may not be able to induce them to give evidence on our side. Mr. Lyon has the honour of the firm to support. Mr. Stavanger's family credit and prosperity would be entirely ruined by the proof of his son's guilt. Wear will stick to the Stavangers if they make a sufficiently high bid for her silence. We must therefore place our reliance on the diamonds, which Hugh Stavanger must have hidden somewhere or other. They will be our salvation if we can show that they have been seen in the scoundrel's possession. I am afraid it is a dangerous thing to do, but there seems to be nothing for it but to follow the man to sea. If he does not come home before eight o'clock, it is hardly likely that the stolen property is here. If he does come home it might almost be safe to arrest him on the chance of finding the things on him. But I dread ruining all by premature action, so implore you to be cautious. Let father watch here with a detective if he likes, but let Hilton go at once to Millwall Dock and keep a sharp look out there. He might perhaps discover the name of the ship Captain Cochrane is commanding, and get a passage in her. If he cannot go as a passenger, he can try, after changing his disguise, to go as cook or steward. Of course he does not know the work, but that is a detail that cannot be taken into consideration when such great issues are at stake.'

ELIZABETH BURGOYNE CORBETT

"Now what do you think of that?" said Miss Cory, folding up the letter, which she had stopped to read by the light of a street lamp.

"I think Annie is a wonderful girl. She seems to think of everything," was Hilton's reply, given in a tone of great disappointment. "But her excellent advice comes too late. Our bird has flown, and it will be almost impossible to discover him tomorrow, since he is sure to keep dark, and we do not even know the name of the ship to which he has been taken."

"Yes, men generally have an idea that women are of no use," Miss Cory said, and her voice had such a triumphant inflection in it that her hearers at once found themselves heartened again. "But in this case they may thank their stars that they have got women to help them."

"We shall only be too glad to thank our stars—the women themselves," quoth Hilton. Whereupon Miss Cory rejoined: "Very prettily said, Mr. Riddell, but you don't know yet what you have to thank me for. I know where young Stavanger is to be found this minute."

"Really?"

"Yes, really and truly."

"But how in the world have you managed it?"

"Well, you see, when Annie's letter arrived, you had already left home, and for a while I was more than a little puzzled as to what was best to be done. But there was no time to spare, and I soon had to come to a decision. Had I come to fetch either of you to go to Millwall, we should have been too late, and had I thought of intercepting either of the Stavangers on the way, my efforts would have been futile. There was but one course open to me, and I adopted it without delay. You and I, John, are about the same size. It being already nightfall, and it being, moreover, very essential that I should not be noticed much myself, I took a liberty with your wardrobe that you must excuse. I haven't seen much of dock life, as you know, but I have an idea, which has proved to be correct, that women, at least respectable women, don't hang about the dock gates at night unless they are on the look out for some particular ship. I am not one to stick at trifles, but I did not want to be mistaken for somebody who wasn't respectable, and I did want to be as unnoticed as possible. So I just got dressed in one of your suits, put my hair out of the way—there isn't much of it—donned a long top-coat and took an old hat, and set off for Millwall. I took the Underground, and changed at Mark Lane. At Fenchurch Street I just caught a train starting for the docks. If I had had to wait there I should have had a fruitless errand, for I lost a little time at the other end hunting about the dock gates, and

I was afraid to attract attention to myself by asking my way. Perhaps you think that I ought to have known it, as I was down there with you last summer to look over one of the ships in which you are a shareholder. But things look very different in the bright sunshine, when you have a lot of friends with you, all bent upon pleasure, from what they do at night, when you are alone and nervous, and fearful alike of being seen yourself or of failing to see those of whom you are in search.

"I am thankful, however, to say that I overcame all obstacles, and I was luckier in my mission than I could have dreamed of, for I had barely got up to the dock gates, when a cab stopped for a moment to put down two men, whom I had little difficulty in recognising as Mr. David Stavanger and his son Hugh. I almost betrayed myself by trying to get too near them, as they questioned the watchman, but I suppose they thought themselves quite safe in that out-of-the-way region, and did not even trouble themselves to speak low, or to notice who stood near them.

"'Do you know where the "Merry Maid" is lying?' asked Mr. Stavanger.

"'Yes, sir, she's lying over there, sir, in that basin; but she's not easy to get at. She's been shifted into the middle of the dock, sir. She was to have sailed this tide, but the bo'sun was telling my mate, a bit since, that none of her stores have come aboard, through the steward not ordering them, and telling the skipper that he had. There's been a jolly row, and the steward had to clear in a hurry tonight, although he had signed articles.'

"'Then I suppose everybody all around is in a tear about it?' put in Hugh Stavanger.

"'Not a bit of it, sir,' was the watchman's reply. 'Why should anybody be vexed except the owners? They are the only losers, having to pay a day's expenses for nothing. The men are nearly all ashore, enjoying themselves a bit longer.'

"'But how are we to get on board, if the ship is in the middle of the dock?'

"'Oh, that's easily managed, sir, when you know how to go about it. Hallo, Jim, just show the gents the way on board the "Merry Maid."'

"'Right you are,' said the individual addressed as Jim. 'Come along, sirs.'

"The next minute the Stavangers were on their way to the ship, and I was trudging back to the station, quite satisfied with the results of my mission, except for one thing. I had kept a sharp look-out on both father and son, but could see that they had no luggage whatever with them. Hugh Stavanger may have the diamonds concealed about him, or, as he is sure to have some luggage of some sort to follow him on board in the morning, the property we want to trace may be sent to him tomorrow. Anyhow, Hilton here, if he can get on board, will make it his business to seek it. He knows where to go, and he ought to start early, as the ship sails about noon. Just to finish my story—I got home as quickly as I could, and changed my clothes. Then I thought that, as you had missed Annie's letter, you would perhaps hang about here all night, on the look-out for Captain Cochrane and his passenger. So I took a cab, and got out in the next street to the one I expected to find you in—and here I am, dead-tired, if I may own the truth."

While Miss Cory had been talking, the trio had been walking homewards. They hoped to have come across a belated cab or hansom by the way, but were not fortunate enough to do so. They were all, therefore, very glad when they reached home, where warmth, food, and rest awaited them.

V

An Old Friend in a New Guise

The ss. "Merry Maid" was making capital progress. She was well-engined, well-manned, her disc was well in evidence, and wind and weather were all that could be desired. The captain was in an unusually good humour, for, in addition to his regular means of making money over and above his salary, he had an extra good speculation on hand, in the shape of a young passenger whose supposed name was Paul Torrens, but whom we have known as Hugh Stavanger.

Mr. Torrens, as we will also call him for a time, hardly looked like the typical fugitive from justice, for his face, as he sat talking to Captain Cochrane, was that of a man who feels exceedingly well pleased with himself. The two men were sitting in the cabin of the steamer. Before them stood bottles and glasses, and the clouded atmosphere of the apartment gave testimony to the supposition that both men were ardent votaries of the goddess Nicotine.

"After all, it's quite jolly to be at sea," observed Mr. Torrens. "I expected to feel no end of squeamish."

To which elegant remark Captain Cochrane replied in kind: "And you haven't turned a hair! I am glad of it too, for I hate to have to do with folk who get sea-sick. They are such an awful nuisance while ill, and are limp and unsociable for days sometimes, even after they are supposed to be over the worst of the visitation. A fellow who can take his share at the whisky bottle is more to my taste."

"Then I ought to suit you?"

"Yes, you do. Perhaps better than you imagine."

"Indeed? I should like to know what you mean. It's something new to be so well appreciated."

"It doesn't take much to please me. Kindred tastes and a well-lined pocket go a long way towards it."

"But if the owner of the well-lined pocket declines to part with the rhino?"

"In this case there is something more at stake than mere rhino, and I think that the present possessor of it will not dare refuse to go shares with me."

As Captain Cochrane said this he emphasised his meaning by such an unmistakably menacing look that Mr. Torrens shrank together as if struck, and grew pale to the very lips.

"Of whom and of what are you speaking?" he stammered. But his whole manner showed that he entertained no doubt on the subject, and his companion was so sure of his position that he did not trouble himself to enter into explanations, but smiled coolly and remarked: "Suppose we go into my berth to discuss matters more fully? It may save future trouble if we come to an understanding at once, and this place is perhaps not quite private enough."

Without a word of remonstrance or comment, Mr. Torrens rose and followed the captain into his private berth. The latter closed the door behind his visitor, and pointed out a comfortable chair to him.

"Now then, we will talk business, Mr.——Torrens. I happen to know that the individual who got potted for a certain diamond robbery had no more to do with the job than I had."

"How do you happen to know that?"

"Well, during the time that elapsed between receiving a visit from a certain Mr. Stavanger, and the reception of his son as a passenger on board the "Merry Maid," I made a good many inquiries which enlightened me considerably. I based my inquiries on the circumstance that it was found desirable to send Mr. Hugh Stavanger out of the country—presumably for his health, which happens to be very good. That little yarn about his declining health turning out to be fiction, I looked around for another reason, since it is evident that a reason there must be. It was not difficult to discover that Mr. Hugh Stavanger had of late been leading a very fast life, and that he had been much more flush of money since the robbery than was the case before that event took place. I am not given to being foolishly charitable in my opinions of others, and I did not think myself to be far wrong in believing that I knew the source of his increased income. There was another thing that convinced me that I was right. There had been no hesitation in fixing the guilt of the robbery upon a man against whom there had never been a breath of suspicion, and who had proved himself a valued servant. The rancour with which such a man was pursued to his doom ought to have set blear-eyed Justice on the right track. But she has such a curious knack of toading to wealth and position that a poor devil in the dock stands no chance at all, but may thank his stars that no more lies are raked up against him. No doubt Messrs. Stavanger felt it to be necessary to secure a conviction, since, the affair being apparently settled, the law's sagacious bloodhounds could turn their attention to a less simple case on the face of it. Perhaps they have not remembered that this Riddell whom they have sent to penal servitude has friends and relations who may even now be trying to find evidence against the real thief."

"And if they are seeking evidence, what has that to do with me?"

"Everything, my dear sir, since it may result in a reversal of your positions. But we have beaten about the bush long enough. It's time we spoke plainly. You are, I am quite sure, the man who stole the diamonds, and swore away another man's liberty to save your own skin. There must be a good share of the stolen property in your possession. In fact, it is in that little leather bag that you take such care of, that it goes to bed with you at night. Too much valuable property is good for no man. You will therefore fetch that bag out of your berth at once. You will then open it, and spread its contents upon this table, the door being securely fastened against intruders. I shall then choose my share of the plunder as a solatium to my conscience for consenting to associate with a thief."

"And what if I refuse?"

"Then I shall have you fastened in the remaining spare berth, without giving you a chance to overhaul your baggage. I shall then have you taken ashore at Malta, and formally charged with being an absconded thief; your baggage will be searched, and you know best whether you can afford to refuse my offer of complete protection, on condition that we go shares in the plunder."

For a few seconds Mr. Torrens did not reply. Then he resigned himself to the inevitable, and, cursing his ill-luck, which left him no peace; cursing his father, who had chosen a scoundrel to convey him out of harm's way; cursing the captain because he was an avaricious brute; cursing anything and everybody but his own vile self, he proceeded to the berth he had occupied during the time he had been at sea. Thence he soon after emerged, carrying the small bag to which Captain Cochrane had referred.

Meanwhile the latter was smiling with satisfaction, and chuckling at the astuteness which was helping him to enrich himself so easily. When Mr. Torrens left him for a moment he felt no uneasiness concerning the diamonds, for he considered that that worldly-wise young man would not throw the proof of his guilt through the window in preference to sharing it with another.

"He is not fool enough to chuck it away, and if he were so inclined, I am keeping a sharp eye on his berth, and can stop him if he even tries to open the bag before he brings it here."

So murmured the captain, quite unconscious of the fact that his low-spoken words found an eager listener. Yet so it was, and to explain how this happened a slight description of the cabin of the "Merry Maid" is necessary.

It was a square apartment, lighted from a large skylight in the centre. On either side it was flanked by berths. To the right, at the foot of the companion, was the steward's pantry. Then came the berth allotted to Mr. Torrens, and those which the officers occupied. Immediately opposite the passenger's berth was the captain's room. On either side of the latter were built respectively a small berth for the steward and a bathroom. Another spare berth on this side completed the accommodation.

The steward was evidently a man with an inquisitive turn of mind, for during the conversation just recorded he was kneeling on the top of his bunk, with his ear pressed close to a small orifice in the partition wall. It was an odd coincidence that the steward, who had shipped under the name of "William Trace," should have a hole at the front of his berth through which he could survey the cabin when desirous of doing so. Still more odd was it that the pantry should also be similarly furnished with means of observation. To prevent undue notice of his own movements, Mr. Trace had furnished his peepholes with small discs of cardboard, with which he covered them when he required a light in his room. The orifices were so small and so cleverly placed as to be almost certain to escape detection, provided the steward was careful.

When we first observe him watching the captain, and listening to his conversation with Mr. Torrens, his face is lighted up with joy, and his limbs are shaking with excitement.

"He cannot escape me," he thinks. "I have run him to earth, and within ten days he will be denounced. Heaven grant me patience to keep my counsel until we reach Malta. Ha! now he returns with his ill-gotten gains, and that other scoundrel little imagines how he will be punished for his greed."

For the next ten minutes Mr. Trace finds connected thought impossible, but, with his eye put close to the peephole, is taking a necessarily circumscribed view of the scene being enacted in the captain's berth. There is a tempting display of very beautiful jewellery, and there is considerable haggling anent its distribution. But the latter is accomplished at last, and the captain places his share in his private desk, which he locks very carefully. Mr. Torrens, wearing a very savage look on his face, crosses the cabin to his own berth, and fastens the door after him. As it is still early in the afternoon, he is perhaps thinking of taking a nap.

The steward is apparently satisfied with his observations for the present, for he gets down from his post of vantage, and prepares himself for his afternoon duties. Tea has to be ready at five o'clock, and, from a purely stewardly point of view, much time has been wasted, so that it behoves him to hurry himself now. His beard, which is brown and bushy, requires some little readjustment, and Captain Cochrane would be considerably surprised if he could see how easily removable both beard and wig are.

But we, who already recognise in William Trace our friend Hilton Riddell, feel no surprise whatever, unless it be at his temerity in offering himself for a post concerning the duties of which he knew positively nothing. When, on attempting to engage a berth as passenger in the "Merry Maid," he found his application rejected, he straightway resolved to change his disguise; and having found that the ship had not her full complement of men, and could not sail until morning, he resolved to apply to the mate to be taken on as steward. The mate, without much inquiry, gave him the post, and had already repented of his indiscretion, for a man may have a great deal of natural aptitude, and yet fail utterly at a post that is quite strange to him. It was so with William Trace, and he had already learnt the savour of a seaman's invective.

It may have hurt his pride a little to hear himself called a fraud and a duffer, and to have a number of burning adjectives hurled at his head everyday. But, in view of his recent discoveries, he is inclined to condone these offences against his self-respect.

Unfortunately for him, he has forgotten to lower the piece of cardboard with which he is wont to cover the peephole which overlooks the captain's berth.

From such simple oversights do tragedies spring.

VI

A MYSTERIOUS DISAPPEARANCE

Late that evening the steward of the "Merry Maid" was sitting in his berth, writing.

The accommodation at his disposal was of the most meagre kind. It included neither desk nor table, for which, by-the-bye, the tiny place would not have had room if they had been available. By way of a substitute, however, his washstand, which was of the sort commonly considered quite luxurious enough for a seafarer, was fitted with a deal top, and upon this he had spread the wherewithal to write a long letter. He sat upon his campstool and applied himself very diligently to his work, covering sheet after sheet with minute writing. Actually, he was writing a very detailed account of all that had transpired after he left home to enter upon the duties of an amateur detective. Having made his budget of news as complete and circumstantial as possible, he folded the papers upon which he had written into a long, thin roll. Then he reached out of the drawer under his bunk an empty wine bottle. He had evidently prepared it for the occasion, for it was quite clean and dry. Into this receptacle he thrust his roll of paper. Then he corked the bottle, and wired the cork firmly down, tying over all a piece of washleather, in order to prevent the possibility of the entrance of sea-water into the bottle. His next proceeding was to open the port, and to lower the bottle through it into the water, through which the "Merry Maid" was running at the rate of ten knots an hour—not at all bad for an ordinary ocean tramp, as the class of vessels to which the "Merry Maid" belonged is often called.

"There," he thought, "I feel easier after taking that precaution. One never knows what may happen, and there is too much at stake to permit it to depend entirely on my safety. I wonder what makes me feel so uneasy. I don't think I have done anything to betray myself. And yet I have a strange foreboding of coming ill. Shall I ever see old England again? Just now I have my doubts. Throwing that bottle into the sea was the first outcome of the new feeling of dread which has come over me, and even if ill comes to me before we reach Malta, there is the chance of Harley being rescued after all, for the first person who picks the bottle up will examine and report upon its contents. I once read of a castaway bottle floating about two years—sent hither and thither, caught first by one current, and then by another—before it was finally washed ashore. God grant that Harley may not have to wait two years for his deliverance."

While he was thus musing in a depressed mood that struck him as uncanny and unaccountable, considering the information that he had gained, the steward of the "Merry Maid" prepared himself for bed, for he had to rise early next morning. Had he but cast his tired eyes up to the little peephole which overlooked the next berth, he would have noticed something which would have alarmed him. The hole being unprotected, the light from his oil lamp had betrayed him.

The captain had retired for the night, but found sleep to be in too fitful and fleetsome a mood to benefit him. The fact that he was richer by at least a thousand pounds than he was a day or two ago had set his imagination going, and he was in fancy entering into all sorts of plans for doubling his capital. Towards one o'clock, he was dozing off, when a slight noise awoke him. Some people are easily aroused by any unexpected sound. Captain Cochrane was one of these people. There is hardly anytime so quiet at sea in a merchant ship as one o'clock in the morning. All hands not on watch are in bed, and those who are on watch content themselves with doing their duty. Supplementary caperings or promenadings are deferred until a more seasonable time.

This being the case, we can understand how it was that Captain Cochrane was on the alert at once when the sound of a splash in the water close to his port fell on his startled ears. For a moment he lay wondering whether someone had fallen overboard or not. Then, just as he came to the conclusion that the splash was hardly loud enough to account for a cat falling into the water, he noticed something else that surprised him.

Just opposite his face, as he sat up in his bunk, there was a small round patch of light. He had no light burning in his berth. Whence came this illumination of a spot to which no light for which he could account could penetrate? He must find out. With Captain Cochrane, to resolve was usually to do. It did not take him long to discover William Trace's secret.

A hole had been deliberately cut in the partition. Such an act would not be done without a purpose. What was that purpose? A very cursory inspection, conducted in the quietest possible manner, convinced the captain that he had come upon a means of espionage. He himself had been the object of supervision. It was time to reverse the situation, and this was accordingly done. The blood of William Trace would, of a surety, have run cold if he could have seen the baleful look in the eye which was now peering down at him as he unconsciously betrayed his dual identity by divesting himself of the thick wig and beard, which he found hot and uncomfortable.

Chancing, as he vaulted into his bunk, to glance at his means of inspecting the next berth, he noticed, to his horror, that the card-board disc was not in its place. To repair the omission was the work of a moment. But he could not so soon recover from the shock which his blunder had caused him. The sense of foreboding which had visited him in the earlier part of the night attacked him with redoubled force, but amid all his doubts of his own personal safety, inspired by his conviction of the villainous character of the two men with whom he had to deal, there rose a sense of thankfulness that Harley's rescue no longer depended entirely upon his brother's personal safety.

The replacing of the card-board disc prevented Captain Cochrane from seeing into the steward's berth. But this fact did not trouble him. The hole had served his purpose, and he had seen enough to convince him that he had brought to sea as ship's steward a man who was neither more nor less than a spy. A spy, moreover, who had found it necessary to cloak his identity by an elaborate disguise.

What could be his special motive, and who was the object of his attentions? The captain felt quite easy as regarded himself, for he had always been very careful to avoid adding to his perquisites in so clumsy a manner as to lead to unpleasant inquiries. His transaction with Mr. Torrens was the first for which he felt the law might have a legitimate grip upon him. But as the steward had evidently been officiating as spy, or detective, whichever he might like to call himself, before the occurrence of the little scene just alluded to, it was clear that this was not the cause of the stranger's presence on board. His motive must be anterior to the division of the spoil. Yet that it had something to do with the flight of Mr. Torrens, and the abduction of the said spoil, Captain Cochrane felt morally convinced.

Now, had the pursuit and discovery of a diamond thief involved no loss or danger to himself, the skipper of the "Merry Maid" would not have felt very much concern. But the events of the last few days had materially altered his notions on the subject. For, whereas he would formerly have felt it incumbent upon him to lend his aid in the cause of right and justice, he now felt his own safety involved in the maintenance of Mr. Torrens's desire to do what he liked with what was left of the proceeds of his venture.

For was he not an accessory after the fact? And had he not in his own possession a very handsome share of the plunder? Detection and exposure of Torrens meant loss, disgrace, and imprisonment for Captain Cochrane.

"Having gone so far," he said, clenching his teeth, and looking very grim about the eyes, "I will go on to the bitter end. I won't allow any man to foil me, if I can help it. This William Trace, as he calls himself, came here at his own risk, and on his head be it if he does not find his way home again."

The next morning, or, rather, at eight o'clock the same morning, there was considerable speculation in the minds of two of the individuals in the cabin of the "Merry Maid." One of them was the steward, who was, to the best of his ability, attending to the wants of those at the breakfast table. But though he was keenly observant of the captain's manner, there was nothing in it that could lead him to suppose his secret to have been betrayed. Nay, the captain was even more forbearing than usual, and had nothing to say anent the sloppy nature of the dry hash, or the extraordinary mixture dignified by the name of curried lobster.

Altogether, breakfast passed over pretty quietly, and Hilton Riddell, alias William Trace, began to feel more comfortable in his mind. Further espionage he did not think necessary to go in for, as he had already learned enough to prove his case. If only the ship could be made to accelerate her speed, and arrive quicker at Malta. He could then disburthen himself of the immense responsibility which weighed upon him. Meanwhile, the best thing he could do was to endeavour to give satisfaction as steward, in order to lead as peaceful a life as possible while on board.

After breakfast, the captain requested Mr. Torrens to accompany him to the chart-room, as he had something he wanted to show him there.

"Certainly; any blessed thing for a change," said the passenger. "I should feel inclined to blow my brains out if I had to put up with this stagnation long. How on earth you fellows stand the monotony, I don't know."

"Well, you see," was the captain's reply, as the two were crossing the poop deck together, "we are used to the life, and, what's more, we like it. But that is not what I want to talk to you about just now. I have something to tell you that will astonish you. Ah! there he goes. Do you know that fellow? I mean the one who has just gone along to the galley."

"Of course I know him. He is the steward."

"So I thought, until last night, when I witnessed a performance not intended for my eyes. That fellow, who has shipped with us as steward, and calls himself William Trace, is a detective, and he is after you."

"Good God! how do you know that?"

"He has got a very good outfit in the way of disguise. That bushy beard of his is false. So is his wig. And I happen to know that he saw you bring the diamonds out of your berth into mine. And that reminds me. I want to have a look into that same berth of yours."

"For God's sake, don't trifle with me. Is what you say about the steward true?"

"Yes, it's true enough, curse him."

"Then I'm lost."

"I don't know about that. Anyhow, I don't mean to give in, and lose what I got last night, without a struggle."

"But what can we do if the thing is found out already?"

"There are a good many things which desperate men can do. But, before we decide anything further, we'll go below again, while our enemy is in the galley."

Suiting the action to the word, the confederates proceeded to Mr. Torrens's berth.

"I thought so," observed the captain; "look here."

"At what? At that little hole into which you have thrust your finger?"

"That little hole is one of the traps that has betrayed you. There is one just like it overlooking my berth."

"But nobody can see through it."

"At present, no. Because it is covered on the other side. Remove the cover, and put an enemy's eye to the hole, and where are your secrets? There is no doubt about it. This fellow has followed you here, and he has now discovered all he came for. It's lucky for you that we went shares last night, for you would have small chance of getting out of the mess by yourself."

"Who will this be? Have you any idea?"

"A detective from Scotland Yard, most likely. Employed by the friends of the man who is in gaol."

"Riddell has a brother who, in my hearing, swore not to let the matter drop. My God, what a fool I am! This is the very man. I wondered what his voice and figure reminded me of. Now I know. This is Harley Riddell's brother himself. He will tell everything when we get to Malta."

"We mustn't let him."

"How are we to prevent him?"

"He must never reach Malta. I tell you, I won't be baulked of my share of the diamonds, and you have far more at stake than I have. It often happens that a man falls overboard."

For a moment the two villains looked into each other's eyes. Then they understood each other, and Hilton Riddell's fate was mapped out before that interview ended.

Somehow, the steward's duties seemed interminable that day, for the captain had taken it into his head that the chart-room required a thorough cleaning and overhauling.

"Steward," he said, "I want you to try what sort of a job you can make of this place. Our last steward didn't half look after things. You can get the engineer's steward to help you for an hour. It won't take you longer than that."

The work might be uncongenial to a man of Hilton Riddell's tastes and temperament. But it had to be done, and he was not one to shirk his responsibilities because they happened to be distasteful. So he occupied himself up in the chart-room, unconscious of the fact that his berth was being searched all over. The searchers found enough to convince them of his real identity. They also made the discovery that it must have been he who wished to sail as passenger in the "Merry Maid," but whom Captain Cochrane, in obedience to Mr. Stavanger's request that he would carry no passenger but Hugh, had declined to take. There was the long red moustache, and there was the checked tweed suit worn by the would-be passenger, whose career was to be so soon ended.

It was singular that the lock of the steward's door should have gone wrong, and that when he went to bed that night he could not turn the key, as was his wont on retiring. "I must put that right tomorrow," he thought. Then, believing himself to be unsuspected, and therefore in no danger, he went to bed, and, being very tired, soon dropped into a sound slumber.

At 12 P.M. the chief mate was waiting impatiently for the second mate to come and relieve him, for he felt as if he could keep his eyes open no longer. The longest spell off watch that the mates of a merchant cargo steamer ever have is four hours. From this four hours must be deducted half an hour for a wash and a meal, leaving three

ELIZABETH BURGOYNE CORBETT

and a half hours as the utmost length of time they have for sleep. As a rule, they no sooner lay their heads upon their pillows than they fall asleep, and the two men who were scheming against the steward's safety meant to take advantage of this fact. To all appearance they had gone to bed. In reality, they were never more keenly on the alert, and, in the absence of both mates, they were tolerably safe, as they knew how to choose their moment for action. They waited until they heard the second mate ascend the companion to relieve his superior. Then they swiftly and noiselessly entered the steward's berth, closing the door after them.

But, careful as their movements had been, they startled the sleeper, who attempted to spring up in his bunk. There was a sudden blow, a stifled cry, and a short but sharp struggle, at the end of which Hilton Riddell lay passive and lifeless in the hands of his assassins, who had deemed strangulation the safest way to silence their victim.

When, about two minutes later, the mate came off watch, all was quiet in the steward's berth. But the two men stood gazing at each other with horror-stricken eyes, and instinctively turned their backs upon the awful object which but a few moments ago had been full of life and strength.

For fully an hour they hardly dared to breathe. Then, feeling sure that the mate must be sound asleep now, they set about removing the evidence of their crime. The captain, who, like his companion, was shoeless for the occasion, slipped up the companion, to reconnoitre.

"All is safe," he presently whispered to his fellow-murderer, who had not dared to remain alone with the body, but had come out into the cabin. "There is not a soul about. The folk on the bridge will be looking in any direction except behind them, where we are. And even if they tried to look this way, the night is too dark for them to see anything."

Soon after this there was lowered, over the side furthest from the mate's berth, the remains of what had been the steward of the "Merry Maid." The body was lowered so carefully, too, that not the slightest splash was caused that could have attracted the attention of an unsuspicious person.

A while later the "Merry Maid" arrived in Malta. Here the captain duly reported the sudden and unaccountable disappearance, of his steward. "The poor fellow was eccentric," he said soberly, and with a great show of sympathy. "He did not drink, but told me that he had once been in a lunatic asylum. The weather was quite clear and calm. He must have had an attack of insanity and jumped overboard. Enemies? Certainly not; he was a general favourite on board."

And so it came to pass that a verdict of suicide while temporarily insane was made to account for the disappearance of William Trace, and his murderers, poor fools, imagined themselves safe from detection.

VII

Evil Tidings

Mrs. Riddell and Miss Cory were sitting in the drawing-room. Both ladies were occupied less fancifully than ladies of fiction generally are. They were darning stockings, and Mrs. Riddell's spectacles were dimmed with tears, as she held up a neatly finished piece of work, and sighed wistfully, "I wonder if poor Harley will live to wear it again."

"Live to wear it!" was the optimistic rejoinder. "Of course he will. He's not particularly ill, though he's naturally low-spirited. But he will soon be all right, when we are able to infuse a little more hope into his mind than is advisable at present."

"Do you know, I was sorely tempted to tell him yesterday of all that is being done for him. It seems so cruel to leave the poor fellow in misery."

"But think how much more dreadful his disappointment will be, if things do not go off so well as we have reason to expect. Far better wait until we hear from Hilton. Then we shall, I trust, have something definite to promise him. Meantime, as you are aware, every effort is being made to trace Hugh Stavanger's doings from the time of the robbery until the time of his flight. Our chain of evidence, with God's help, will soon be complete, and when we have effected his deliverance, we will all do our best to make up to your poor lad for some of his sufferings."

"I wish I could feel as you do. But, somehow, as each day passes, I begin to lose heart more and more, and yesterday, when I saw my dear boy, looking so ill and miserable, I thought my heart would have broken."

"Yes, I knew you would feel it keenly, and wanted you to stay at home. Perhaps it is as well that you will not be permitted to see him again—until honour and freedom are restored to him. Picture how happy we shall all be then!"

"I will try, dear kind friends, I will try. And what do I not owe you already! Without you to hearten me up, when I am tempted to doubt Providence, I should have fretted myself into my grave before this time. But don't you think we should have the telegram which Hilton promised to send from Malta soon? Shouldn't it be here today or tomorrow?"

"I suppose it should. Only we must, of course, make allowances for possible bad weather and other causes of detention."

"Yes, yes, I won't be impatient again."

Mrs. Riddell, utterly crushed by the suddenness and severity of her recent troubles, was prone to despondency and melancholy. It was fortunate for her that she had found such a firm, cheerful, and hopeful friend as Miss Cory to cheer her now childless loneliness. Annie, too, though she took her lover's fate sadly to heart, was fain to do her utmost to keep up the health and spirits of both herself and others.

"There may be important work before me," she was apt to say, "and I should feel ashamed of myself if I were to allow myself to become incapable of doing it."

So she kept herself fully occupied with healthy employment, took her food regularly, and held herself in readiness for action at any moment. On the afternoon during which the above conversation took place between Mrs. Riddell and Miss Cory, Annie had been with her father to see a private detective whom they were employing to make inquiries concerning Hugh Stavanger. But although the man gleaned proofs that the individual whose past he was trying to investigate had spent a great deal of money lately, he could discover nothing to connect him with the diamond robbery.

"Never mind," said Annie bravely, as they were walking homewards again. "We shall hear from Hilton soon, and he is not likely to lose sight of Hugh Stavanger, so that he can be arrested as soon as we are ready with our proofs. When Mr. Lyon comes home, we will have him subpœnaed as a witness, whether he likes it or not."

"I don't think we can rely upon him," said Mr. Cory.

"And I do think that we can. I have given him a good deal of consideration, and have come to the conclusion that he is a gentleman. From the inquiries we have made of him, we have learnt nothing that could lead us to believe him anything but honourable. A few days ago I thought as you do. Mr. Lyon has no doubt every desire to shield the honour of his firm. But when he comes back, I mean to interview him and implore him to help us to save an innocent man from worse than death."

"And surely he cannot refuse so reasonable a prayer."

"I wonder how he came to suspect Hugh Stavanger, and how much he really knows."

"We shall, I hope, discover everything in time—at any rate, enough to reverse the positions of Harley and young Stavanger."

"Poor Harley. How dreadfully ill he looked yesterday! And yet how brave he tried to be! But hurry up, father, you know that it is just possible

ELIZABETH BURGOYNE CORBETT

for the 'Merry Maid' to have reached Malta today, and a message may even now be waiting for us."

There was no cablegram waiting for them, but the quartette spent the rest of the day without augmented anxiety, little dreaming of the terrible tidings in store for them. Late in the evening they were all sitting round the drawing-room fire, the ladies working while Mr. Cory read extracts from the "Echo."

"Great Heavens!" he exclaimed suddenly, as his eye lighted on a passage which filled him with consternation. "Surely God himself is working for our enemies."

His words so startled his companions that at least two of them were incapable of inquiring the nature of the new calamity which had evidently befallen them.

"What has happened now?" gasped Miss Cory, her face pale with consternation.

"Read for yourself," was the reply, as her brother handed the paper to her. She took it with trembling fingers, but gained courage, when she saw, at a glance, that the news was not what she had feared.

"Don't be so alarmed, Mrs. Riddell," she said reassuringly. "This paragraph does not concern your son." Then she read aloud as follows:—

TERRIBLE COLLISION AT SEA.
GREAT LOSS OF LIFE.

"The news of a painful disaster has reached us from New York. The Pioneer liner 'Cartouche' reports a collision between that vessel and the British steamer 'Gazelle' on the 31st ultimo. The weather was thick at the time of the collision, and the foghorn of the 'Cartouche' was blowing. Suddenly a vessel emerged from the fog, and was seen to be crossing the starboard bow of the 'Cartouche.' The latter was immediately ported, and her engines set full speed astern. But these efforts could not prevent a collision, and in a few seconds the 'Gazelle' was struck amidships, going down immediately, with every soul on board. Some of these were afterwards picked up by the boats of the 'Cartouche.' But 28 persons are known to have perished, among these being three first-class passengers—Mr. Thomas Ackland, the Lancashire cotton spinner; Mr. Henry Teasdale, son of the Member for Sheffington; and Mr. Edward Lyon, junior member of the firm of Stavanger, Stavanger and Co., diamond merchants, Hatton Garden."

For awhile there reigned an awestruck silence in the room.

"There seems no doubt about it," at last said Mr. Cory.

"No, the information is positive enough," was his sister's response.

"It seems dreadful," said Annie, with quivering lips and streaming eyes, "to think of oneself when reading of such awful catastrophes. The news is sad enough for anyone to read, but how can we help thinking also how strangely it affects us? Wear is dead; and now death has overtaken the only other witness, apart from ourselves, upon whom we could hope to place any reliance. Surely God must have forsaken us altogether."

"Not that, my dear child," was Mrs. Riddell's trembling protest. "We are sorely tried. But I cannot bring myself to think that He has wholly deserted us. He is just trying us to the utmost of our strength."

With this, Mrs. Riddell stooped to kiss Annie. Then, wishing the others "goodnight," she left them, for she feared to break down, and thus increase the sorrow of the others. She also hoped that her Bible, a never-failing source of comfort, would lend her its tranquillising aid. Alas, she was soon to experience a trial great enough to make even her faith falter.

The next morning all four were seated at breakfast, when a servant brought the morning paper in.

"Quick, father," said Annie. "Look at the shipping news and see if there is any account of the 'Merry Maid'."

Mr. Cory turned obediently to the part of the paper named. But he was so long in making any remark that Annie looked up in surprise, which deepened into terror when she saw the expression of her father's face. It was white and drawn, and big drops of perspiration stood upon his forehead.

Mutely she asked to see for herself what was the new trouble sent them. And mutely he handed her the paper. The reader already knows what she was likely to read there, and will not care to witness the grief with which the news of Hilton Riddell's death was received.

But, great though the grief was, there came a time when other passions gave it battle.

"My boy has been murdered," said the heartbroken mother. "I may lie down, and die. Hilton is dead, and Harley's last hope is gone."

"Hilton has been murdered," said Annie. "But Harley's last hope has not gone. I still count for something, and I will never rest until I have tracked and denounced the man to whom we owe all our misery."

"Hilton has been murdered," said Mr. Cory. "But the world is not so very big after all, and I swear that his murder shall not go unavenged."

"Yes, there has been murder," said Miss Cory; "and everything must be done to punish the fiend who is guilty of it. I cannot go with you, my place is with our unhappy friend here. But I can do this much—I can place my fortune at your disposal. Spend it freely in tracking our enemy. I will give every penny I have for such a purpose. Go, and my blessing go with you."

So far, everything had seemed to work in Hugh Stavanger's favour. All those whom he had to fear were swept from his path. But, if he had heard and seen what passed at the Corys, he would perhaps have trembled.

And he would have had good cause for trembling. For Nemesis is not an agreeable foe to follow in one's wake.

VIII

On the Track

A splendid mail steamer, bound for the Orient, was ploughing its way through the notoriously treacherous waters of the Bay of Biscay, whose surface today was of the brightest and calmest. There was little to indicate the horrors of which "The Bay," as it is called by sailors, is so often the witness, and most of the passengers were congregated about the deck, chatting, reading, smoking, or otherwise doing their best to enjoy the leisure hours at their disposal.

"So this is the dreaded Bay of Biscay again," said Mrs. Colbrook, a stout, good-humoured-looking lady. "I suppose I am exceptionally lucky, for it has always been smooth when I crossed it."

The persons she addressed were Mr. Cory and Miss Annie Cory, who, however, had thought it advisable to take their passage under the names of Mr. and Miss Waine. They were bound upon an important errand, and did not intend to risk failure by proclaiming their identity too widely. True, the chances that anyone knowing their motive in voyaging to Malta would come across them by the way were so remote as to be almost beyond the need of consideration. But Mr. Cory was so far cut out for detective work that he was not likely to fail through lack of carefulness, and preferred to neglect not the smallest precaution.

"Yes, Mrs. Colbrook," he smiled, in reply to that lady's remark. "There is little to indicate the mischief that goes on here sometimes. We may be thankful that we are favoured with such beautiful weather."

"That we may! I cannot picture anything more awful than to be in a ship at sea in a storm so bad that destruction is almost certain," said Annie. "It seems to me to be like no other danger. On land there is always some loophole of escape if the peril is of a protracted nature. But on the wide, trackless ocean, with not another ship in sight, things look almost hopeless from the first. I have more than once tried to picture the terror and distress that must reign on board a doomed vessel, but my mind faints before the awful picture."

"There I think you are entirely wrong," remarked Mrs. Colbrook. "I believe that awful panics on board sinking ships are of much less frequent occurrence than is generally imagined."

"And your reason for that belief?" asked Annie.

"A little experience of my own. I was, a year or two ago, on board a small steamer bound from the Tyne to Antwerp. There were only five first-class passengers, all of them ladies. We had but been at sea about three hours when a terrific storm arose, which speedily threatened to sink our ship. The wind howled, the rain poured in torrents, the lightning flashed, the thunder rolled, the ship played such a fine game at pitch and toss, that everything breakable was smashed to atoms, and we seemed to be oftener standing on our heads than on our heels, or would have been, if we had been able to stand at all. Soon after the storm began the steamer's wooden deck groaned and creaked awfully, and the timbers, as if afraid that we were not fully realising the dangers of our position, considerably gaped in a score of places, so that whether we were in our bunks, or whether we were in the saloon, it was all the same—we were so copiously supplied with the elemental fluid that our clothes and bedding were saturated. Three of the ladies sat, shivering and miserable, holding on to the cabin table, and hoping for the advent of the steward with news of a probable improvement in the weather. Near them sat the stewardess, in as helpless a condition as they were. Even if she had cared to risk an attempt to go on deck, she could not have done so, as we were battened down, there being some fear lest the little ship, in her crazy pitchings and rollings, would ship the cabin full of water and swamp us all. Cooking and attendance were all postponed for the time being, 'for,' as the stewardess coolly remarked, 'what was the use of trying to prepare a meal if you were to be drowned directly afterwards?'

"Three of the passengers, including myself, were lying in bunks, so sick and ill that we could do nothing whatever. I do not know whether I was worse than the others or not, but it is certain that I was too helpless to lift the eau-de-Cologne bottle that was lying by my side, although I longed for the use of some of its contents, thinking that it might, perhaps, help to remove the deadly faintness by which I was overpowered. After several hours of this misery the steward came to us for a minute, but did not render us any service. Asked by the stewardess what was thought of the chances of survival by those on deck, he replied that pretty nearly everybody on deck looked for the end every minute. Then we were left to our own reflections again.

"Now this was the time when a panic would have been the most likely to arise, since it was the moment when we practically lost all hope. But, strange as it may seem, the four women at the table sat as quietly as before, and two of them, who were sisters, calmly wondered how the news of their death would be received at home. The other two were crying quietly, and spoke very little. The three sick ones, beyond an occasional moan of misery, gave no outward token of having realised their apparently speedily approaching end, and the only thing that I now longed for was that the steamer, if she was going to sink, would be quick about it, so that my misery would be at an end."

"And you were not drowned after all?" queried Annie, with a spice of mischief in her voice.

"No, we were not drowned after all—but, look there, how excited all those people seem to be."

Mr. Cory and his daughter followed the direction of Mrs. Colbrook's eyes, and saw that quite a crowd of people were gathering on the starboard bow, whence some object of interest ahead seemed to be engaging their attention. Our friends soon became members of the curious crowd, and were saddened by the spectacle pointed out to them. It was the battered and mastless hull of a derelict ship, floating on the now smooth waters, and presenting mute evidence of their whilom relentless fury.[1]

Glasses were hurriedly brought into use, and countless conjectures as to the name, nationality, and experiences of the wreck were hazarded. Not a sign of life was perceptible on its deck, and it was all too evident that the crew no longer found a home in it. As to their fate, who could say what it had been? Perhaps they had been saved by some passing vessel. Perhaps they had been swept into the seething and roaring waters, their last shrieks rendered inaudible by the war of the elements. Perhaps, imagining their battered ship to be sinking, they had succeeded in taking to the boats, and might be even now floating on this billowy waste, with the pangs of hunger and thirst gnawing at their vitals, and with "water, water everywhere, and not a drop to drink." Perhaps—but why lose oneself in endless painful conjectures, since a solution of the questions that puzzle us is out of our power to arrive at?

To Mr. Cory and Annie the sight was especially painful, for it brought vividly to their minds poor Hilton's fate, and they could not help picturing the last scene of his life as an awful one. This only

---

1. It may be argued by seafarers that the Bay of Biscay is out of the track of derelicts. This supposition is, upon the whole, correct. But there are exceptions to every rule, and at the time of writing there is marked in charts a derelict off Lisbon.—The Author.

strengthened their determination to avenge his untimely end, and the sad conjectures with which the fast approaching wreck was greeted were mingled with a feeling of bitterness at the misery and suffering which were permitted to run riot upon the earth.

"No," said Annie, after a lengthened pause in the conversation, during which she seemed to have divined her father's thoughts; "we mustn't lose faith, after all. Please God, all will come right yet. Those scoundrels will be brought to book, and Harley will be proved innocent. Then we shall all be happy again."

"Meanwhile, though, Harley is suffering untold misery; Mrs. Riddell seems to be fretting herself into her grave; Hilton has met with a violent end; and Providence seems to be doing its best to help the cause of villainy."

"Yes, it is difficult to understand. But the cause of the wicked cannot always prosper, and the tangled skein of our destiny will unravel itself in time."

"So I suppose. We can only hope that the thread of our life doesn't snap before then. One doesn't like to feel as if one were so much the sport of fate, as to be like a mere cork on the ocean of life, tossed about with as little ceremony as—as—as that bottle."

Mr. Cory had found himself somewhat at a loss for a suitable simile, when his eyes fell on a bottle lightly tossing on the rippling water.

"I suppose that bottle is carefully corked, or it would fill with water and sink," observed Annie, contemplatively.

"Yes, I should imagine it has papers in it," said her father, "unless somebody has corked and sealed an empty bottle for a freak."

Both speakers knew of the practice of confiding news concerning sinking or endangered ships to papers sealed in bottles, and felt a subdued interest in the black little object bobbing about the water. How their interest would have been quickened could they have known how Hilton had employed his last night on board the "Merry Maid," and could they have dreamed that this was perhaps the very bottle whose contents were intended to be instrumental in proving who was really guilty of the great diamond robbery, for the perpetration of which Harley was enduring penal servitude. But so it is. We often strive for the unattainable, and pass our greatest blessings by with indifference.

The derelict ship was by this time quite near, and scores of eager eyes were scanning it, to see if perchance there was not after all someone left on board. But all looked as quiet and deserted as when the wreck had been first sighted, and it was with many a sigh of pity that the hope of still saving some of the crew was abandoned. There had been many suggestions from passengers that the mail boat should slow down, and send some men to board the derelict. But this proposal was negatived by the captain, as he did not believe anybody was on board, and was not justified in losing time for mere curiosity's sake.

So the great steamer forged ahead, leaving the stranger in its wake, and it was already well astern, when suddenly a long, mournful howl was heard, thrilling every soul on board with a feeling of horror. Once more eyes and glasses were brought into requisition, and then it was seen that a large dog, or, rather, the emaciated skeleton of one, was tottering to and fro on the poop of the dismasted wreck, and howling forth a pitiful appeal for succour to the possible saviours whom, in the semi-obliviousness of exhaustion and starvation, he had failed to see when nearer.

"You will stop the ship now, won't you?" cried out a dozen people at once. But the captain declined to do any such thing.

"I have my reputation for speed and efficiency to keep up," he said. "I have no end of competition to fight against, and I cannot afford to lose time for a dog's sake."

"Oh, how can you be so cruel?" exclaimed a bright, fair girl, of about Annie's age. "It will be as bad as murder if you refuse to save the poor beast. Oh! listen."

Again that long-drawn howl of despair escaped the distracted and suffering animal, as he saw that the distance between himself and an ark of safety was rapidly widening, and there were others who joined their entreaties once more to those of Miss Bywater.

But the captain's resolve was adamantine, and loud murmurs of disapproval were heard on all sides, while many of the ladies could not refrain from crying, so powerfully was their pity and excitement aroused. Mr. Cory's face was also twitching with sympathy, and his hands were clenched angrily, until the conduct of the dog put an idea into his head upon which he at once based his action.

Seeing that the steamer was leaving him to certain death, the brave beast flung himself into the water, determined upon making an effort to reach the vanishing asylum. Of course, the feat was hopeless, for, though he might have been a good swimmer, starvation had reduced him to such straits, that it was problematical if he would be able to swim twenty yards.

"Annie, I cannot stand this," said Mr. Cory, hurriedly. "You mustn't be alarmed at what I'm going to do. You know that few swimmers can beat me, and if I can save that dog, I mean to do it."

The next moment he had thrown off his coat and waistcoat, and before anyone quite realised what he was about to do, he had dived into the water, and, with swift and powerful strokes, was making for the struggling dog. Instantly there was a tremendous commotion, and the cry of "Man overboard!" resounded from end to end of the mighty vessel, while orders to reverse the engines and to lower a boat were issued immediately. What was refused for the sake of a mere dog, dared not be denied to a man, and every effort was at once made to overtake the plucky swimmer, who was swiftly nearing the object he was striking for. A boat was manned and lowered with astonishing quickness, and amid the suppressed cries of some, and the encouraging shouts of others, the rowers bent to their work, and gave speedy promise of succour. What a race for life that was! And what a shout went up from the deck of the ocean racer when Mr. Cory was seen to reach the dog, which must have been at its last gasp when he seized it, for it was limp and motionless now. This was deemed a very fortunate thing by the spectators, some of whom had feared that the drowning animal's struggles might impede the rescuer's movements. A few minutes more, and the boat reached the plucky swimmer, who, together with the dog, was hauled in, amid the enthusiastic plaudits of the excited onlookers, many of whom, however, thought that help for the starving animal had come too late.

But Mr. Cory had no notion of giving up hope, and clung tenaciously to his prize, although assured that it was dead. And so it seemed for a time, but there were plenty of people willing to aid in completing the good work, and as much pains was bestowed upon the resuscitation of the insensible brute as if it had been a human being. When at last the poor thing opened its eyes, the joy on board the steamer was almost unanimous, and if the ship's surgeon had not asserted his rights, it would have been forthwith killed with kindness, inasmuch as it would have been plied with food which its stomach was too weak to take.

Meanwhile, the vessel proceeded on her way, as soon as the boat was hoisted up, and Mr. Cory went to change his wet clothes for dry ones. When he came on deck again sometime later he was rejoiced to find that the dog, which he forthwith christened "Briny," was making steady progress towards recovery, and that he was already, after his own fashion, giving grateful acknowledgment of the attentions lavished upon him by

Annie and the surgeon. He proved to be a large Newfoundland, and would, no doubt, soon recover his wonted size, strength, and beauty.

The only person who looked coldly on Mr. Cory after this exploit was the captain, who could not forgive the trick that had been played upon him, and who would not have deemed the lives of twenty dogs a sufficient equivalent for the loss of time spent in saving them.

Mrs. Colbrook was a middle-aged lady, the wife of an officer stationed at Malta. She had been in England to visit a daughter, and to see after a legacy which she had unexpectedly succeeded to. She and the Corys had fraternised from the beginning of the voyage, and as time passed she learned to respect them more and more.

"You are only bound for Malta, at present," she said one day. "And you tell me that the business which takes you there may compel you to leave the place directly. My husband will be delighted to know you, and if you will stay with us while you are in Malta you will confer a favour on us both."

"You are very kind," said Mr. Cory, "and it would certainly be much pleasanter for us than staying in an hotel. But I could not think of trespassing upon your hospitality to such an extent without making you acquainted with the object of our visit to the place."

"I do not think that at all necessary."

"But I do, in justice to you. And as I am sure we can trust you thoroughly, I will at once tell our story to you. You will be interested in it, and will the better realise how it is that Annie is at times so sad and preoccupied. She has had some painful experiences, poor child."

And forthwith Mr. Cory confided to Mrs. Colbrook the whole history of the diamond robbery and its disastrous consequences, and found her henceforth all that he had expected—sympathetic, kind, discreet, and helpful. To Annie she was as one of the kindest of mothers, and the girl found it a great comfort to be able to talk of her troubles to one who took such a friendly interest in her, and had such firm faith in the truth of all her statements.

At Malta Major Colbrook met his wife on board the steamer, and his attention was speedily directed to the new friends she had made. As soon as he learned Annie's story and object he was all eagerness to help her, and promised to make some inquiries on Mr. Cory's behalf respecting the man of whom he was in search.

The day after Malta was reached there was quite a merry party gathered at the house of Major Colbrook, for various friends had dropped in to hear Mrs. Colbrook's English news, and to congratulate her on her return home. The Corys, on second thoughts, had preferred to put up at an hotel, but readily promised to spend all their spare time with the Colbrooks. They were both feeling somewhat preoccupied, but did their best to present as cheerful a front to strangers as possible.

Inquiries promptly made had resulted in the following information:— The "Merry Maid" had discharged her cargo of Government stores, and had proceeded to Sicily, leaving behind a gentleman who had come out from England as a passenger. This gentleman's name was Paul Torrens, and it was believed that he was now in Spain. Being aware of the facility offered to criminals by the lack of an extradition treaty between England and Spain, Mr. Cory was inclined to think the supposition correct, but felt reluctant to leave Malta without feeling sure that the man he was tracking had really left the island. Annie hardly knew what to think. At one time she was all anxiety to be gone, and the next moment she was oppressed by an uneasy feeling that to quit Malta at once would be to diverge from the trail. It will, therefore, be readily supposed that their thoughts refused to concentrate themselves on the topics of conversation current in Mrs. Colbrook's drawing-room. Annie, at last, considering that she had done enough homage to conventionality, rose to leave, asking Mrs. Colbrook to excuse her, as she really did not feel equal to remaining inactive.

"You won't be offended if I leave you now?" she pleaded in a low voice. "I seem to be wasting my time unless I am making some progress in Harley's cause, and I am sure my father, for my sake, is just as eager for progress as I am."

"To be sure, dear child," said Mrs. Colbrook caressingly. "I can quite enter into your feelings, and would rather help you than hinder you. So don't consider me at all, but go at once if you really feel that you can employ your time to more purpose."

Mr. Cory was just as anxious to forego the pleasures of polite society as Annie was, so the pair took their leave unobtrusively, and walked towards their hotel. Oddly enough, however, their thoughts now reverted to a conversation to which they had but listened inattentively awhile ago.

"I suppose the Colbrooks and some of their afternoon callers will be going to see this balloon ascent they were talking of," said Mr. Cory, after walking some distance in apparent deep contemplation of a more serious subject.

"Really father," was Annie's rejoinder, "I should have been surprised to hear you talking about balloons and kindred subjects just now, were it not that something else surprises me still more. While Captain Drummond was talking so enthusiastically about this wonderful aeronaut, I did not feel the slightest interest in the subject. In fact, I didn't consciously listen to the conversation. And yet, when you spoke just now, I was actually feeling a desire to witness the forthcoming ascent. I am not quite sure that there isn't something uncanny about it, for I have often had opportunities of witnessing similar displays, and haven't cared to go to them. Today, when it would seem to be sheer waste of time, I feel irresistibly impelled to go and watch the performance of this much-talked-of balloonist. An absurd fancy, isn't it?"

"I am not so sure of that, Annie. I can recall many instances in which I have been unaccountably induced to act contrary to my original intention, and have been glad afterwards that I yielded to an apparently freakish impulse of the moment. Here is a case in point: About twelve months ago certain shares were being boomed sky-high, and so much percentage was being derived from them that I, in common with many other people, decided to share in the general prosperity. As, perhaps, you know, both your aunt and I lost a great deal of money through buying some shares in a big brewery company, which, though about two millions were foolishly paid for it by the dupes who formed the limited liability company which took it over, turned out to be simply an unlimited fraud. The original proprietors had, by dint of advertisements and paragraphs, increased the public confidence in their concern at the very time when it was tottering for support. It was by way of retrieving our losses in connection with the brewery shares that I wanted to profit by buying rising mining shares, and I proceeded to the office of a well-known stockbroker, in order to negotiate without delay. I found Mr.——engaged six deep, and sat down to await my turn to go into his inner sanctum, but had not been seated there three minutes when a strange thing happened. It was as if someone had suddenly whispered to me, saying, 'Get out of this office while you are still well off. Don't trust to this boom.' I gave myself no time to think, either one way or the other, but at once took my departure, saying to the clerk that I would call another time. I have so far not called to see Mr.——, and the much-boomed shares are just worth so much waste paper."

"Then you don't think my fancy to see the balloon ascent an absurd one?"

"By no means. There may be something in it. Anyhow, we will go. But there is plenty of time to spare."

"Then what do you say to going first to such shops as there are, and trying to find out if Hugh Stavanger has been raising money on any of his plunder?"

"A capital idea! I should not have thought of it. I'm afraid you will have to depend more upon yourself than upon me for inspiration. What do you say, Briny?"

Briny was fast getting into condition now, and a great affection had sprung up between him and his new owners, who were bent upon always taking him out with them whenever it was practicable, as he was likely to prove a good protector. An hour was now devoted to doing as Annie had suggested, but without getting any idea of Hugh Stavanger's present whereabouts. One thing, however, they did learn. There was one man to whom two men had offered some diamonds for sale a week ago. The dealer, not being in a large way of business, had not come to terms with the strangers.

"To tell the truth," he said, "they were too avaricious. One of the men was, I think, a ship's captain. The other was a landsman, and I think he must be in the trade, for he knows as much about precious stones as I do. He knew the exact value of the things he had to offer me, and he wouldn't take the highest offer I was prepared to make. But he promised to call back again, and as I think he was very anxious in reality to turn his stones into cash, I have been expecting him to come and close with my offer. If, as I gather from your inquiries, the diamonds have been stolen, I am very glad I did not buy them, for the affair might have ruined me."

"And I am very sorry you did not get them," said Annie, eagerly. "If he comes back, secure the diamonds at his price. We will buy them from you, and will give you a liberal commission for your trouble. The man who has been here was the principal witness against an innocent man, who is now in prison. It is our mission to bring the guilt home to the right party, in the person of the son of the diamond merchant, who professed to have been robbed by a Mr. Riddell. If we can prove him to be possessed of the property, we can prove the innocence of Mr. Riddell. You will help us, will you not?"

"I will do my best, madam. You will find me discreet and silent, and I hope to be able to help in the good work."

"And, meanwhile, here is a banker's reference," said Mr. Cory. "And you may rely upon finding us profoundly grateful if you help us to solve this painful mystery."

"Is the accused gentleman a relative of yours?" asked the jeweller, hesitatingly, as if afraid that he was taking too much liberty.

"He is my daughter's fiancé."

"Ah, now I understand your earnestness in the matter. But how about the seafaring man?"

"I expect it is the captain of the 'Merry Maid,' the steamer in which Hugh Stavanger sailed. If he also had diamonds to dispose of, we may conclude that they are part of the stolen property, and that it is as important to find him as it is to find the original thief."

"He said the ship was sailing next day, so you won't find him in Malta."

"No; but we can follow. But, in any case, don't let Stavanger slip through your fingers if he turns up here again."

A few more preliminaries were settled with the friendly jeweller, and then, prior to going to their hotel for dinner, our amateur detectives went to see the balloon ascent, which was to take place at six o'clock. There was a tolerable muster in the enclosure, and considerable local interest seemed to be shown in the event. The aeronaut was a man of great experience, and had an assistant in whom he had every confidence. The conversation with the jeweller had taken up so much time that our two friends only arrived a few minutes before the order to "leave go" was given, and had not seen many of the preparations. Besides the aeronaut and his assistants, the car was to contain two passengers, both of whom had paid ten pounds for the privilege, and neither of whom had ever been up in a balloon before. Some of the onlookers were betting upon the results, and there was considerable diversity of opinion as to where the descent would take place.

Presently the ropes were let loose, and the ponderous machine rose rapidly into the air, amid the plaudits of the assembled crowd. Mr. Cory was looking on quietly, when his interest became suddenly excited by one of the objects which bobbed over the edge of the car. He looked at Annie in astonishment, to note that she also was gazing breathlessly at the now fast rising balloon.

"We have him at last!" whispered Mr. Cory, joyfully.

"God be thanked, Harley will soon be free!" said Annie, the tears of joy running down her cheeks.

Perhaps their confidence was rather premature, but it was easy to comprehend. For they had both recognised one of the faces looking down at them as that of Hugh Stavanger.

IX

A Balloon Adventure

Mr. Blume, the chief mate of the ss. "Centurion," was pacing the bridge in anything but an angelic mood, which evidenced itself in perpetual growls at everybody with whom he came into contact. The objects of his displeasure, seeing no adequate reason for it, were not disposed to take his fault-finding too meekly, the result being that the atmosphere on board the "Centurion" was decidedly unpleasant.

"I'll bet my bottom dollar that the mate got jilted last time he was in port," remarked the second mate to the third engineer, both being off watch together.

"What makes you think that?"

"Oh, lots of things. He was as jolly as any of us when we first got in, and was perfectly killing when he went ashore to see Lottie, as he always has done whenever we have been in Cardiff. He came back much sooner than usual, in a vile temper, and hardly ever went ashore again. Since we left he has been awfully ill-natured, and I am sure Lottie is at the bottom of it."

"Perhaps she's ill."

"Perhaps she's fiddlesticks. Much more likely is it that she's found another admirer. Lightly come, lightly go, you know. He's a very nice fellow when he likes. But he's only a mate. And if Lottie can see her way clear to pick up a skipper as easily as she picked up our mate, I reckon the poorest man has the least chance."

"Well, if that's what's the matter with him, I'm sorry for him. I've been jilted a time or two myself, and I know what it feels like. I don't think I'll ever look at a woman again with a view to matrimony."

"I say, how old are you?"

"Twenty-two. But I've had experience enough for forty-two, and—"

"Now don't try to kid me anymore. What about that photograph that hangs over your bunk?"

"Oh, that's my sister Nellie."

"Does your sister Nellie write on all her photographs—'To my darling Jim, from his faithful Dora?'"

"Look here. You have been poking your nose where you had no business to poke it. What about yourself?"

"My dear fellow, I never saw the woman yet that I would tie myself to."

"You pretend you don't like them?"

"Nothing of the sort; I worship them. But I believe in variety, and prefer to carry a light heart from one port to another."

"How does variety affect your pocket?"

"Very conveniently. I admire only respectable girls, and they never know me long enough to prove expensive. Hello, what's up now?"

As the second mate made this exclamation, he turned his eyes to what seemed to be an object of speculation to many on board. It was trailing along the water a considerable distance ahead, and was as yet somewhat difficult to distinguish. On the bridge the mate was also exercising his mind about it.

"I can't make the thing out," he said to the man at the wheel. "It can't be a boat of any sort; and yet, what else would you expect to see scudding on the water before the wind like that? Here, have a look, Greenaway; your eyes can see further than mine."

Greenaway did as he was bid, and, after careful observation, remarked quietly, "It's a dismasted balloon, sir, and there are some fellows hanging on to the rigging."

"A dismasted balloon! What the deuce do you mean?"

"Well, sir, I mean what I say. She's dismasted. Leastways, her sail's flopping about anyhow, and doesn't help her a bit. I reckon it's about time them fellows took to their boats. If they don't they'll soon be exploring Davy Jones's locker."

"I always knew you to be a blamed fool, Greenaway; but, hang me, if you don't get worse. What makes you call the thing a balloon?"

"Why, I reckon I call it a balloon because it is a balloon. I don't see that you can have a better reason, sir. Hello! One of the fellows has tumbled overboard. I fancy there isn't much chance for him. By Jove! one of 'em's jumped down on deck, and hauled him in again. Are we likely to overtake them? I would like to cheat old Davy."

By this time Mr. Blume had seized the glasses, and, being now much nearer, could see for himself that the battered and wave-tossed object before him was a balloon in reality, though how its occupants came to be in such a plight he could but faintly conjecture.

"Run and tell the skipper," he cried eagerly. Then, knowing beforehand what the captain would do, he ordered the man at the wheel to steer for the distressed aeronauts. In another minute the captain was on deck, having been just about ready to sit down to his breakfast. He fully endorsed the mate's action, for he was not one to refuse succour to victims of the elements.

"Stand by to lower a boat," he shouted, his order being promptly carried out. When sufficiently near for the purpose the boat was lowered, and her crew soon had the satisfaction of rescuing four exhausted men from the aerial vessel, which, relieved of their weight, slowly rose into the air, and floated southwards in the direction of the African coast.

The condition of the rescued men was truly pitiable, and they were saved none too soon. They had a painful story of peril to relate as soon as warmth, food, and rest had done their beneficent work.

"When we made our ascent from Valetta," said the captain of the balloon, "the wind was just as I had hoped for it to be, and the people who saw us ascend had little conception of what was before us. Some seemed to imagine that the descent would take place within a few score yards of the place whence we ascended. But I knew better, although I little dreamed of the experience really in store for us. There was not much chance of landing on shore, and I expected to travel a short distance out to sea, and to be picked up, after a simple ducking, by a steamer which I had chartered to follow the balloon. But shortly after leaving the coast-line we noticed that the wind had gained strength, and was carrying us southwards at a rapid rate. Our water anchor was useful for a time, but unfortunately the rope broke; we lost our anchor; and the balloon rose several hundred yards.

"Soon, however, a terrific downpour of rain caused us to descend again, and the balloon was dragged along the surface of the sea. We were now in a very sorry plight, for the car was frequently under water, and we had to cling desperately to the ropes to save ourselves from drowning. We must all have perished hours ago, but for the courage of Mr. Calderon, my assistant, who made frequent dives into the car, and brought up the ballast, one bag at a time, an expedient which only raised the balloon by occasional fits and starts. We next threw away the greater part of our clothing, which was sodden and heavy with rain and sea-water. Even our money and the only bottle of spirits we had went overboard, for life itself depended on our being lightened to the utmost. In this connection I cannot refrain from animadverting on the conduct of Mr. Torrens, one of our passengers. He threw his coat overboard, but declined to part with anymore of his clothes, even though very strongly urged to do so. Once, numbed with cold and fatigue, he lost his hold of the rope to which he was clinging, and fell into the sea. He will never be nearer death than he was at that moment, for, lightened of his weight, the balloon began to right itself, and we firmly believe that it would have risen and carried us to a place of safety, if we could have reconciled ourselves to abandoning him to his fate.

"The temptation to do so was a terrible one, I assure you.

"'If we leave him to drown we shall be saved.'

"'If we rescue him for the present we shall probably all be drowned.'

"'His life is worth less than all ours. Why should we die to save him?'

"These were the thoughts that assailed us, and of the three left hanging on to the balloon I am sure that none but Mr. Calderon would have mustered courage and self-denial sufficient to go to the rescue of Torrens, who was drowning fast, he not being able to swim at all.

"We had sighted a great many ships during the night, but were unable to attract the attention of any of them, as we had no light. When day dawned things looked more hopeful, but your help came none too soon, for we were all about dead beat."

Such was the story of the captain of the balloon, related to the captain of the ss. "Centurion," and afterwards published in all the principal newspapers of Europe. I may add that these published accounts were supplemented by the grateful acknowledgments of the aeronauts for the kindness and attention shown them by those on board the "Centurion." At Alexandria the steamer, which was en route for Madras, discharged its passengers, who at once proceeded to arrange for passages elsewhere.

The two professional aeronauts and their Maltese passenger returned to Valetta, but the gentleman unfavourably known as Mr. Torrens preferred to disport himself in fresh fields and pastures new. One of his principal reasons for not returning to Malta was due to a fright he got when leaving that place. As he rose in the car, feeling perfectly secure against pursuit and detection, and elated by the enjoyment of his novel position, he looked down at the sea of faces below him, and was startled to recognise Miss Cory, whom he knew again as the young lady who was figuring as his sister's governess when he left home.

Like a flash the truth struck him. "She is shadowing me," he thought. "I believe it is the girl whom I heard was engaged to Riddell. If so, her presence, first in my father's house, and then here, bodes me no good, and the sooner I clear out the better. I hope the machine won't be in too big a hurry to drop, so that I shall have a chance of getting away. It's lucky I got that belt to carry my property in. It's much better than either pockets or a bag, and I have left nothing at my lodgings that I need worry about. Hang it, why can't I be left to enjoy myself without a lot of meddling fools coming after me?"

"You don't feel upset, do you?" inquired his fellow-passenger, noticing that Mr. Torrens had grown somewhat pale and frightened looking.

"Well, you know, it's a queer sensation, mounting up here. Still, I shall be all right in a minute."

So said he, feeling glad that so natural an explanation of his confusion was at hand. But he had no intention of being seen at Valetta again, and when, his balloon adventure over, he was cast upon his own resources in Alexandria, he deemed it desirable to think of someother place to which to proceed. There were certain difficulties in the way. But these must be promptly overcome. For if, as he feared, the face he had seen at Valetta was that of an enemy and pursuer, it behoved him to quit Alexandria before the landing place of the rescued aeronauts became too widely known. Unfortunately, all the money he had with him had been in the pocket of the coat he was compelled to throw into the sea. His refusal to doff his waistcoat when urged to do so arose from the fact that it as well as the belt had some valuable diamonds stitched into its lining, and he preferred the risk of drowning to the certainty of poverty.

It was with some reluctance that he found it necessary to try and negotiate the sale of some of his incriminatory property. For anything he knew telegrams might have been exchanged already, and the myrmidons of the law might even now be on his track. Still he could not manage without money, so the risk must be run.

He did run the risk, and though his identity was quite unsuspected by the dealer, he found himself compelled to accept half the value of the stone he offered for sale, or go without money. He was naturally a good bargainer, and it stung him to the quick to feel himself outdone. "But what can't be cured must be endured" is an axiom which sometimes impresses itself painfully upon us all, and as Mr. Hugh Stavanger, alias Paul Torrens, was no exception to the general rule, he found animadversion useless.

That evening, after writing a long letter to his father apprising him of both his present and his intended whereabouts, he became a passenger on a steamer bound for Bombay, having booked his passage under the name of Harry Staley, as he considered "Paul Torrens" to be no longer a safe appellation.

X

A Bright Pair

Letter from MR. STAVANGER to his SON.
(Written in Cypher)

My Dear Boy,

"For you are my dear boy still, although you have of late caused me a great deal of anxiety. You hardly know how much I endured until I received your letter from Malta, and even then I was tormented by a dread of what it might have been found necessary to do. I allude to the death of the steward, which, to say the least, was very lucky for us. You wonder how I know this? I will tell you later on. There is so much to relate that I must start at the beginning, or I shall get mixed up. First and foremost, the business is steadily recovering from the shock given to it by the abstraction of so much portable property. Secondly, my brother has not the slightest suspicion that there is any reason why Harley Riddell should not stay where he is, and I am beginning to be of his opinion. This belief is inspired in me by a strange sequence of circumstances, all of which seem to point to one conclusion. He must really be a very wicked man, or Providence would not work so persistently against him as it seems to do. Everything that could help him and hurt you is almost miraculously rendered powerless, and everybody whom we had cause to dread has been promptly removed. How, therefore, can anyone doubt that Divine vengeance is exacting atonement for some fearful crime which has not yet been brought to light? This being so, we are nothing less than the instruments used by Providence for its own ends, and I regard what you have done as the involuntary outcome of an inexplicable and unconscious cerebral influence.

"But now that the aims of Providence are achieved, I beseech you to assert your own identity and to fight against any impulse to repeat anyone of the dangerous proceedings of the past few months.

"And now for such news as I have. Perhaps I ought to have mentioned sooner that your mother and sisters are quite well. Also that I am in like case both mentally and bodily, now that I know you to be rid of your enemies. It would have been an awful Damoclean sword hanging over us if that inquisitive Wear had not been providentially removed from our path. Then there was my poor old friend Mr. Edward Lyon. Did you see in the papers anything about his sudden death while away on his business mission to America? I had nothing but esteem for him. But I must say that I felt immensely relieved when the news of his death reached us. He had turned unpleasantly suspicious just before he sailed, and would most assuredly have begun to make undesirable inquiries on his return. But heaven has seen fit to remove him to a better world. That it has at the same time removed one who might have been the means of proving Riddell not guilty of the crime for which he suffers is only another proof to me that he is, as I said before, being made to expiate some former sin.

"Nor is this by any means all the proof of my theory. You know Clement Corney? And perhaps you feel uneasy at the mention of his name. If so, you may set your fears at rest, for he also is numbered among those who might have been a witness against you, but is not. A week ago he came to me with a long tale about what he knew and about what he suspected. You seem to have been imprudently confidential with him, and to have allowed him to pry into your affairs far too much. From what he told me I judged him to be a very formidable witness against you and deemed it advisable to accede to his demands for money, but looked with anything but equanimity upon the prospect of having to continue supplying him with money as long as he chose to blackmail me. I should have been left no choice in the matter, as exposure, after having gone so far, would mean ruin. But here Providence once more interposed most strangely. Last night, on opening my evening paper, I came upon the account of the inquest on Clement Corney's body. He had been jerked from the top step of a 'bus and had broken his neck.

"This is all very strange and wonderful. But the strangest thing of all has to be related yet. As you will see by the postmark of this letter, we have come to St. Ives for our holiday. We arrived here on Monday, and on Tuesday I was walking on the beach and wondering how you were going on when I saw a group of children become considerably excited. Going up to them I found that one of them was holding a bottle which had been washed up by the tide. Seeing that the bottle was carefully sealed, and appeared to contain papers, I offered the children a shilling for it. They ran off with the shilling in high glee, while I secreted the bottle in my dustcoat, and walked rapidly towards our lodgings with it. I cannot account for the impulse which prompted these apparently irrelevant actions, except upon the hypothesis of Providential interference already mentioned. I do not usually take much interest in the doings of children, and I am not naturally of a prying, inquisitive disposition, and yet I was anxious to open that bottle in the privacy of my own bedroom. And now mark the result.

"That bottle contained papers giving a detailed account of all that Hilton Riddell, alias William Trace, had done, and was doing, to ruin you and liberate his brother. What a sneak the fellow has been to deceive people, and to do the tricky things he was doing. No wonder he came to a bad end. And how vindictive he must have been to write down all he wrote on the papers that have so wonderfully been put in my possession. Why, only one half the details would have reversed the relative positions of his brother and yourself, if anyone but me had secured that bottle. It seems miraculous, doesn't it, that, after tossing about on the waters of the broad Atlantic, the fragile receptacle of a deadly secret should have been guided to the only person who knew how to make a proper use of it? I broke the bottle, and after reading them destroyed the papers. And what do you to say to the strange fact that I, who had never been in St. Ives before, should chance to be there just when that bottle was washed ashore? Only picture what a calamity it would have been had anyone but myself stumbled upon it.

"The whole thing has only served to strengthen the belief expressed nearer the beginning of this letter, and I no longer feel the slightest qualms of conscience on his behalf.

Nor do I feel much further uneasiness about you. Wear is dead. Mr. Lyon is dead. Clement Corney is dead. The carefully-prepared proofs against you which Hilton Riddell consigned to the waves have perished in a more deadly element, and he himself is powerless to do you further injury unless the sea gives up its dead. All things taken together, therefore, you may consider yourself perfectly safe, and I do not think there would be the slightest risk in your returning to England, and resuming your duties at the shop. Let me know as soon as possible whether you intend to do so or not. You will have had sufficient holiday, and ought to try to make up for all the worry you have caused me lately.

"One thing puzzles me a little. How did Hilton Riddell get to know that you were sailing in the 'Merry Maid,' and what led him to pitch his suspicions on you? It couldn't be all chance, and, but for his timely extinction things might have been very awkward for you by this time.

"But enough of this subject. You know all there is to know, and I know as much as I want to know. Nor do I desire ever to open the subject again.

"You will be interested to hear that Mr. Leonard Claridge is violently in love with Ada, and is very anxious to marry her off-hand. I am just as anxious that the marriage should take place as he is, for it would be a great thing to have Ada so advantageously settled. She pretends to turn her nose up at an offer from a grocer. But she is a very sensible girl, after all, and will reflect that if Mr. Claridge is a grocer he is not in the retail line, and will be able to provide her with an establishment quite equal to her mother's.

"Fanny is likely to be much more troublesome to us. She is very passionate and intractable, and nobody seems able to manage her since the night you left home. That night was also the one on which Wear came to such a sudden and tragic end. It was also the night on which that governess disappeared, who seemed to have such a genius for managing Fanny. When I returned home, after seeing you safe on board the 'Merry Maid,' the governess had gone out. It was odd that she never came back, wasn't it?"

Yes, it was certainly odd. Indeed, it was the one fly in Mr. Stavanger's ointment. Just now the fact did not trouble him, because he was not aware of it.

At one of the principal hotels in Bombay a young man sat reading the letter from which the above long extract is given. He would have been fairly good-looking but for the unpleasant expression which his reckless indulgence in vicious pleasures and his aggressively selfish temperament had given him. In height and breadth he somewhat exceeded the average, but his gait was seen to be clumsy when he walked, although his proportions were regular enough. His hands and feet were small and well shaped, his complexion of a clear, but healthy enough paleness when he condescended to lead an abstemious life. Just now it was full of tell-tale pimples. His features were regular; his teeth well-shaped, but slightly discoloured; his hair, eyes, and expression all as black as they can be found anywhere.

Such was Hugh Stavanger, known on the hotel books as Harry Staley. He had been to the "poste restante" for his letter, and as his eyes wandered from one page to another, rapidly deciphering the contents that would have proved so baffling to anyone not initiated in the business of Stavanger, Stavanger, and Co., the heavy scowl on his face gave way to a look of evil triumph, not unmingled with astonishment.

"Well, of all the lucky accidents, these beat everything," he murmured. "To think of all those people being bowled over like that. But what a caution the governor is, to be sure, with his talk about wickedness and Providence. And he really writes as if he believes what he preaches. There is one thing, though, in which he is quite right. The sea can't give up its dead, at any rate not in such a condition as to be able to speak against me. Hullo! What's this? Curse that girl. There is no mistake about her now. She was a spy when pretending to be governess. She disappeared from our house the night I sailed. This means that she found out where I was going to, and set that scoundrel of a Riddell on my trail. Her next manœuvre was to follow me out to Malta. These people evidently know who really took the diamonds. And they are moving heaven and earth to bring me to book. Ah! well! They mean to win. So do I, and all the odds are now in my favour. They may suspect what they like, but they haven't a proof left. As the governor says, Providence is dead against them. We all know that it's no use flying in the face of Providence, so my enemies are foredoomed to disappointment.

"So the governor thinks I had better go home again, and that I should be quite safe. I don't exactly agree with him, and I have an idea that I can work a trick worth two of that. This interesting young lady, whom I imagine to be Miss Cory, wants to discover my whereabouts. I have, very foolishly, been running away from her. I think I will reverse my tactics. It would be completing the good offices of Providence if I were to permit my enemies to overtake me. Nay, I will go further than that. I will give them indirect information of my whereabouts. Then, just when they imagine the hour of their triumph has arrived, I will remove them from my path with even less compunction than I felt over Hilton Riddell.

"Yes, the hunted shall turn hunter, and whether it is God or devil that is helping me, I mean to win."

XI

An Unexpected Ally

Annie trembled violently when she saw Hugh Stavanger disappearing with the balloon, and for a moment seemed almost fainting with excitement.

"Courage, my darling," said her father. "He can hardly escape us now, for I will at once take steps to have him arrested as soon as the balloon descends. Now your desire to see this balloon ascent is partially accounted for. Oh, here is Major Colbrook. Do you know, sir, the man of whom we are in search is actually in that balloon?"

"Are you sure?"

"Quite sure. We have taken note of his appearance too closely to mistake any other man for him. We have also heard some news about him this afternoon, and have secured a witness who saw him with the stolen diamonds in his possession."

"By jove, you are getting on. I suppose there had better be no time lost in seeing after his capture as soon as the balloon descends. But where, in the name of fortune, is it going to? Why—it's going right out to sea!"

Others had noticed also that a catastrophe seemed to be impending, and intense excitement prevailed, which became augmented when the balloon was lost sight of altogether. As we know, darkness came on while the aeronauts were still being whirled away from the steamer which was to have overtaken them, and they would have perished but for the opportune arrival of the ss. "Centurion."

The Corys were dreadfully disappointed at this fresh freak of fate. To lose their prize when it seemed so nearly within their grasp was a blow sufficient to shake their hope of ever being able to help Harley, for everything worked against them.

"I am afraid your chances of laying your hands on Stavanger, junior, are gone," said Major Colbrook, when he called to see our friends the next morning.

"How so?" inquired Mr. Cory.

"Well, none of the ships that have come in this morning have sighted the balloon. The probability is that it has come to grief, and that the men are all drowned or killed. I am sorry for the other fellows, but sympathy would be wasted on a scoundrel who would swear another man's liberty away for a crime he has committed himself."

"Perhaps so. But, if Stavanger has perished, the proofs of his guilt will have been lost with him, and that will be a very serious thing for us."

"But you have a witness in the shape of the jeweller, who can prove that the diamonds were offered to him for sale."

"There you are wrong. Unless we can secure some of them, we cannot show reasonable proof that these are the identical diamonds that were stolen."

"I think, father, that the sooner we look after that ship-captain the better. You know we were told that he also had some jewels for sale. As he was in Hugh Stavanger's company, I expect he had exacted them as the price of his silence or his help. If we can find him, it may turn out that we can do without the diamond merchant's son. Our present object must be to expedite Harley's liberation. The punishment of the wrong-doers can follow after."

"Bravo, Miss Cory. You have hit the nail on the head," exclaimed the major. "Look here, we know the name of the ship, and that she has left Malta. Let's go to the harbour-master, and find out where she cleared for. You may be able to catch her at the next discharging port. Before you could overtake the 'Merry Maid' now she will be loaded and away. So you must find out somehow where she is bound for."

As Major Colbrook's advice was considered good, it was acted upon at once, but the result of the inquiries made was somewhat disappointing. The "Merry Maid" had gone to Barcelona, and from there to Gibraltar for orders, and what those orders were would take some little time to discover.

"Have you the 'Shipping Gazette'?" inquired the major.

"No, sir; we don't go in for that much, and I have no recent copies by me. I'll tell you what, though; if it is very important that you should know where the 'Merry Maid' is, why don't you cable to the owners?"

"A very good idea, if I knew where to cable to," said Mr. Cory. "But I have not the slightest notion who the owners are."

"There I am better informed than you," put in Annie, eagerly. "Hilton gave me the name and address of the owners, and I have them here in my note-book."

"Capital!" cried the major. "We shall manage it yet. Now for the address."

"Messrs. Rose and Gibney, agents, Great Water Street, London."

"Good. The next thing is to decide what to say. You don't want your own name to figure, I suppose? No? I thought not. Then you had better cable in my name, and direct the reply to come to my house."

After a little delay, the following message was sent to Messrs. Rose and Gibney:—"At what port, and when, is 'Merry Maid' due?"

The answer to this, which had been prepaid, was—"Due at Cardiff, 4th proximo, from Antwerp, to load for Port Said."

"Splendid. That will suit you to a T," exclaimed the major. "You can stay here two or three weeks, to give yourself time to hunt up as much information as possible about Stavanger. Then, failing success, you can proceed from here direct to Port Said, and board the 'Merry Maid' in the canal. By the time you get to Cardiff, the vessel might have started on her voyage, so your surest chance of success lies in waiting for this Captain Cochrane at his port of destination. And I think you had better take the authorities into your confidence. They might help you to find Stavanger."

It was agreed to follow Major Colbrook's advice in the main, but our friends preferred to go on to Port Said without much more delay.

"Hugh Stavanger probably saw us," said Annie. "If so, he will not come back to Malta."

"Perhaps not, but you have no guarantee that your supposition as to his having seen you is correct. And you will surely not leave here till news of some sort respecting the balloonists arrives."

"No; it will be better to wait a little while."

That a little patience was advisable, was proved when the particulars of the rescue of the balloonists came to hand. When, however, the Corys learned that Hugh Stavanger was not returning to Malta, they left the island for Port Said as soon as it could be managed. But here they were baffled again, as by the time they landed, the man whom they sought was already on his way to Bombay, and no efforts of theirs could discover a trace of him.

"We must remain here now until the 'Merry Maid' arrives," said Annie. "Meanwhile, it strikes me that we have been acting very clumsily. To give a different name to ship captains and hotel proprietors is not enough. We must disguise ourselves effectually. It is quite possible that Hugh Stavanger recognised me at Valetta, and that but for that misfortune he would have been brought to book by this time. Such a blunder must not be made again. We have a great stake to play for, and we intend to win."

"You are right, Annie. If the fellow suspects us, he will look out for us, so we must circumvent him by losing ourselves, as it were."

The result of the conversation that now ensued between father and daughter was a complete change in the appearance of both of them, and those who could recognise Mr. Cory or his daughter in the elderly clergyman who was supposed to be the tutor and travelling guide of the rather delicate-looking young Englishman who accompanied him would have to be extremely wide-awake. There was no cessation of watchfulness on the part of the so-called Rev. Alexander Bootle and Mr. Ernest Fraser. But very little that was of special interest to them occurred during their stay in Port Said, and they were very glad when at last the "Merry Maid" appeared in the port. Duly armed with the necessary authority, the Rev. Mr. Bootle, accompanied by an officer of the law, went on board the steamer the moment it was possible to do so, his object being the arrest of Captain Cochrane, on the charge of being accessory after the fact to the great diamond robbery in Hatton Garden.

Picture his dismay on discovering that Captain Cochrane had not come out with his ship this time. According to the account of Mr. Gerard, the new master of the "Merry Maid," Mr. Cochrane had had a legacy of a thousand pounds left him lately, and he had resolved to take a holiday for the space of a voyage. On the return of the ship to England, he meant to join it, and Captain Gerard would then have to subside into his former position of chief mate.

That evening, conceiving that nothing was to be done there towards the object they had at heart, Mr. Fraser and his companion were arranging their luggage, preparatory to returning to England on the morrow. Both were downcast—the former particularly so.

"It's of no use trying to do anything for Harley," was Mr. Fraser's remark. "The way in which we are foiled at every turn is driving me mad. Surely fate cannot always work so determinedly against people who are fighting on the side of right and justice."

"I don't know. It's a queerly mixed-up world. But I don't see any cause for being so terribly disheartened. We may come across Cochrane in England without much trouble. And it is just possible that Stavanger has gone back to England, too. He may think himself safe there now, and events may develop rapidly in our favour while there."

At this juncture, a knock was heard at the door, and a servant entered the room with a note on a salver. The note was brief, but puzzling.

"The present captain of the 'Merry Maid' would like an interview with the Rev. Mr. Bootle. He thinks that Mr. Bootle will be greatly benefited thereby."

"Show the gentleman in," was the order given as soon as the note was read, and a moment afterwards a tall, well-made man entered the room. He was about thirty years old, originally possessed of fair hair and a concomitant complexion. Already, however, his hair was of the sparsest, and of nondescript tint, while exposure to the weather had invested his face and neck with the ruddiest of hues. As if to atone for the lack of hair on the top of his head, he was endowed with a moustache of which nine men out of ten would have envied him the possession. The extremely punctilious neatness of his attire would have led many to set him down as foppishly inclined. But one look at the keen, piercing grey eyes would have negatived the supposition that he was of a weak nature.

"Pray be seated, Captain Gerard," said Mr. Bootle. "You have business with us, I believe."

"Well, I think so. To begin with, you don't seem to be friendly towards Captain Cochrane."

"One isn't usually good chums with the people one wants to arrest."

"Precisely so. Now, I am not particularly anxious, either to do Cochrane an ill turn, or to do you a good turn without sufficient reason. A short explanation of my position will show you that I have a strong personal motive in seeking your further acquaintance. I have been ten years in the employment of the owners of the 'Merry Maid,' and when two years ago I passed my final exam., and got a master's ticket, I was promised the first vacancy as captain that offered in the company. Soon after this the former skipper of the 'Merry Maid' died, and I expected to be appointed to her, but was disgusted to find myself passed over in favour of a cousin of one of the owners—Cochrane, forsooth. Now, he is a man with not half my experience, and is popular with nobody that has to sail with him; so you may readily believe that I have not found it easy to swallow humble pie as his subordinate. At present he is taking a holiday. He says that he has had a legacy left him. You boarded the ship this morning with a warrant to arrest him on a charge of being concerned in a diamond robbery. I have put two and two together, and have come to the conclusion that the legacy is a hoax invented to cover his possession of money he could not otherwise give a good account of. If your suspicions, and my suspicions, I may add, are proved correct, Captain Cochrane won't tread the 'Merry Maid's' deck again. Failing his return, I am sure to be given permanent command, and as I consider myself to have a right to the position, I shall be very glad to give any information I can that will remove my rival from my path. I have, you see, been perfectly straightforward and honest with you. I don't pretend to disinterested motives, or any rot about only being anxious to serve the ends of justice. I want Cochrane out of my way, and for that reason alone I am ready to co-operate with you against him. If you care to give me your confidence, we may be able to help each other."

Both his hearers had listened eagerly to what Captain Gerard had to say. Then they nodded to each other, after mutually questioning the advisability of trusting this stranger, who might, after all, be a friend of Captain Cochrane, and might have come to pump them in order to put the villain on his guard. But, somehow, they were both inclined to believe what had just been told them, and renewed hope coursed through their veins at the prospect of making important discoveries after all.

"I believe what you say," remarked the Rev. Mr. Bootle, after a short pause; "and after you have heard all there is to say on our side, you will, I am sure, be even more ready than at present to help us."

Then followed a recapitulation of all the details already familiar to the reader, and it was as Mr. Bootle had surmised. Captain Gerard became greatly excited, and vowed that he would do all he could in the cause of justice, even if it became imperative to work openly, and thus lose the favour of his employers, who were Cochrane's relations.

"And you say that Riddell's brother sailed as steward in the 'Merry Maid' last voyage? Depend upon it, he must have betrayed his identity in some way or other. And I will tell you why I think so. There has been some whispering aboard the ship about the late steward's disappearance. If this steward was the man you say, his disappearance is no longer mysterious. He was murdered. And, what's more, I will try to prove it."

BAITING THE TRAP

Y̶ou would like to know my reasons for believing that your friend has met with foul play," said Captain Gerard, after the first horror and surprise of his hearers was over. "Well, here they are. It was only yesterday that our second mate, who is new to the ship, related a conversation he had had with the bo'sun. The latter asserts that on the night that saw the last of the man supposed to be William Trace, it was so unbearably stuffy down below that he coiled himself up beside the winch, between the third and after hatch, and went to sleep there. He says that it must have been approaching morning, when he suddenly awoke with a sensation of danger, such as we all experience at times when our sleep is disturbed. With his senses all on the alert, he looked about him, without at first noting anything. Then it struck him that the sound he had heard was a splash, and a moment after he saw Messrs. Cochrane and Torrens creeping stealthily towards the companion, down which they vanished. Shortly afterwards he fell asleep again, and did not connect the steward's disappearance with the splash he had heard, or with the skipper's stealthy movements, until he heard different members of the crew whispering their suspicions of foul play. Had the weather been bad, or had the steward been an unsteady man, it might have been supposed that he had fallen overboard while drunk, as the ship was not rolling. But the man was as steady as the weather was fine, and he could not have fallen overboard without deliberately trying to do so. The inference, therefore, is in favour of his having been pitched over. You may not think this much proof of my belief that he was murdered. But our Chippy stumbled upon a motive, or what would have struck a keen observer as a good equivalent for one. He was ordered by the captain to repair sundry holes which had been made in the wainscoting by the steward. Since I know who the steward was, I am sure these holes had been made for purposes of espionage; that he discovered collusion between Cochrane and the passenger; that they, in their turn, discovered who he was, and deliberately negatived his evidence against them by murdering him. There are also many other corroborative little incidents to be unearthed, I am sure, and I promise you that by the time the 'Merry

Maid' has finished this voyage, there will have been gathered by me all the information possible concerning this suspected murder. Meanwhile, your best course will be to return to England, and try to secure Cochrane. He lives in Disraeli Road, Forest Gate, London. Before we separate I will give you his complete address."

"Is he married?"

"He has been, but his wife is dead. Since her death he has placed his son under the care of a sister, and he makes her house his home also when in port. Only secure him, and you will learn enough to liberate your friend from gaol. Cochrane will tell all he can about Stavanger to screen himself. He is notoriously of a sneakish disposition. If money is no object, I would suggest that you cable to somebody in England to see that the fellow does not give you the slip. And now I guess I had better be moving, as soon as you have given me an address that will always find you. We are going on to Bombay from here. Should I come across Stavanger, you may bet your bottom dollar that I will ensure his arrest."

A few weeks after the above conversation, an elderly gentleman in clerical garb was having a somewhat heated discussion with a private detective.

"How in the world could you bungle so seriously as to let the man slip through your fingers? I telegraphed the importance of his capture to you, warning you always to keep him in sight. And yet I find, on arriving here myself, that you have lost all trace of him."

So said the irate clergyman, to whom the detective replied—

"My dear sir, when you have lived a little longer, you will perhaps have a better understanding of the difficulties of my profession. The man whom I did watch tallied exactly with the description of the man I was instructed to watch, and it is not my fault that it turns out to be the brother-in-law whom I have shadowed. I do not believe Cochrane has been near the house."

"Perhaps you are right. But my vexation is none the less, for, somehow, every effort I have made, so far, has resulted in nothing but disappointment."

"Well, it's a long lane that never has a turning, and Cochrane is evidently dubious as to his safety and has chosen to obliterate himself for a while. We may take it for granted that he won't join the 'Merry Maid' again. Nor will the share of the stolen diamonds which he was seen with at Valetta be enough to support him permanently. I should imagine he will change his name and set up in someother line of business in London or its vicinity. If you care to empower me to do so, I will employ one of my men to investigate, and report the appearance of the proprietors of new enterprises, preferably those of a quiet, shady nature."

"London is such a big place, that we are as likely to stumble across our man in the street, as to discover him in the way you suggest. But I suppose it will be as well to be watchful."

It was only too true. Once more, when apparently on the eve of success, our friends had been most bitterly disappointed by the discovery that their quarry had escaped them. For a week his whilom home was carefully watched, but he did not put in an appearance there, and, after awhile, it was discovered that his relatives were greatly distressed about him, as he had neither visited them nor acquainted them with his place of abode for sometime past.

All things considered, Harley's prospects of release seemed no better than they were at the time of his conviction. But it was at least a little satisfactory to learn that his health had so far not suffered quite so much as had been feared. His mother, too, bore up wonderfully under all her trials, and expressed her firm faith in the ultimate restoration of her son's liberty and reputation. Hilton's fate had been a great blow to her at first. Then, much to the surprise of friends, she declined to believe that he was really dead, in spite of the evidence that was forthcoming to that effect.

"Depend upon it," she said, "God wouldn't be so cruel as to deprive me of both my boys. I shall yet see them happy and well."

After a time nobody tried to argue her out of this belief, for it comforted her, and kept her from sinking into the despondency that would otherwise have overwhelmed her. Miss Margaret Cory was, as usual, a comfort and a consolation to everybody. Mr. Cory was glad to be at home again, but was as determined as ever to pursue his investigations further. Annie—quiet, subdued, and sad—was yet unremittent in her efforts to gain information likely to be useful. As time wore on, she became more brave, nay, positively daring, and showed such skill in safely following up clues that her father no longer felt any uneasiness about her, even though her absences from home were often unexpectedly lengthened.

The family had removed to a new house in a neighbourhood to which they were strange, and none but themselves knew that she was a daughter of the house, since, for prudential reasons, she had retained her masculine clothing, without which it would not have been so easy for her to penetrate unobserved into all sorts of places. Of course the case had been put into the hands of an official detective, who, however, was as much at a standstill as they were.

One day Annie, whom the servants and neighbours supposed to be Mr. Edgar Bootle, son of the Rev. Alexander Bootle, found among the letters on the breakfast table one bearing the Bombay postmark. She concluded at once that it was from Captain Gerard, as he had promised to write on his arrival at Bombay.

"Look here, father," she said eagerly, as the "Rev. Mr. Bootle" entered the breakfast room, "here is Captain Gerard's letter. Open it at once and see what he says."

The request was promptly obeyed, and what was in the letter is here transcribed:—

SS. 'Merry Maid,' Bombay

Dear Sir,

"As per promise, I am losing no time in affording you such information as is in my power. I find that the look-out man who was on duty on the night, and at the time of Mr. Hilton Riddell's disappearance, is also convinced that he heard a suspicious splash, but it is doubtful if either he or the carpenter would care to appear as witnesses in the event of a new trial, since they are afraid of being detained, without recompense sufficient, long enough to cause them to lose their ship. Perhaps, however, you may be able to make them an offer good enough to overcome hesitation in this direction. But I have, nevertheless, some very valuable information for you. Yesterday, having only been in port an hour or two, and having finished all business for the day, I was having a turn on the Apollo Bunda, when whom should I meet face to face but our late passenger. He recognised me at once as the former mate of the 'Merry Maid,' but would have passed by without apparent recognition if I had not buttonholed him, and made this course impossible. He acknowledged my salutation very stiffly, and would still have passed on had I not remarked, 'Look here, old man, it's lucky for you we have met; otherwise you would most certainly be in gaol tomorrow.'

"You should have seen his face. It went as white as a scared man's face ever can, and for a moment he looked as if he was going into a fit. Then he pulled himself together, and tried to make light of his emotion.

"'What a queer way you have of talking, Mr. Gerard,' he said, and I was viciously glad to see what a feeble show he made of the self-possession he tried to muster. 'How on earth could I be entitled to lodgings in gaol?'

"'Well, thereby hangs a tale,' I said. 'Suppose you come down with me to a quiet house I know of, where we can talk unobserved. You have some deadly enemies in Bombay at this minute, and the sooner you take yourself away from a public place like this the better.'

"Fifteen minutes later we were sitting, each armed with a whisky and soda, in the public room of a house which I, in common with other sea-faring officers, had often frequented during my numerous voyages to Bombay. Stavanger was desperately nervous, and was careful to sit with his back to the general company, while I, having a good view of all who came in, was able to assure him that, so far, none of his enemies were present. And then I exercised a stroke of diplomacy, for which I am sure you will commend me.

"I have induced him to set off for England, where you will have no difficulty of capturing him. I set a trap for him, and he has walked into it beautifully. Briefly, this is what I did. I told him that at Port Said a middle-aged gentleman and his daughter, accompanied by an officer of the law, came on board the 'Merry Maid' with a warrant for the arrest of one Hugh Stavanger, alias Paul Torrens, on a charge of being the principal person implicated in a diamond robbery that had taken place sometime ago at Hatton Garden. 'The young lady,' I continued, 'was engaged to be married to a man who has been convicted of the crime, and she has vowed to unearth you and haul you up, if she has to follow you all over the world. She has tracked you from one place to another, and is quite confident of catching you sometime. I suggested that you were probably in England again. But neither she nor her father thought this possible.' 'Depend upon it,' Miss Cory said, 'the scoundrel will never dare come to England again, and it would be folly to look for him there. If he had felt safe there, he would not have come away, that is true.' I told Stavanger much more than this, all tending to make him believe that, after all, England was the only safe place for him. I enlarged on the wealth at your disposal, and said that you had several detectives trying to find him somewhere abroad. Also that you had found out somehow that he had sailed for Bombay, that you had immediately decided to follow him in one of the mail boats, and that you must have reached Bombay a few days before the 'Merry Maid' arrived. I also professed to have no sympathy with you, and remarked that if I could lay my hands on a few diamonds I would only be too glad of the chance. The fellow did not condescend to chum with me at all when I was only a mate. Now he seems to repent his error of judgment; is convinced that I am quite in harmony and sympathy with him; and is ready to swallow any advice that I may offer. Here is the result of my advice and manœuvring. He went back to his hotel with his hat over his eyes, and his light coat huddled about his neck as much as possible, I being kind enough to accompany him. Then he put a few things into his pockets, packed a portmanteau, paid his hotel bill, and went with me to the skipper of a boat leaving for England that tide. He is now a passenger in that boat, which is called the 'Hornby Cross,' and is due in London a month from date. Before parting from him, I, partially by wheedling, partially by insistence, got a diamond ring out of him. This ring I will bring home with me, and, should it prove to be a part of the stolen property, you will have proof enough to saddle the robbery on Stavanger, even if he were not walking right into your clutches. This letter will reach you a week before the 'Hornby Cross' is due, and will give you time to make the necessary arrangements for capture. The 'Hornby Cross' is owned by Messrs. Ward, Willow, and Co., Fenchurch Street, and Stavanger's present alias is John Morton. A word or two more. The scoundrel had half a notion for a few minutes of remaining here, on the chance of being able to 'stop your gallop,' as he called it. In other words, if he can ever get half a chance he will murder you, as he considers that if the world were rid of Miss Cory and her father he would be perfectly safe. I persuaded him that it would be foolish for him to linger here, and vowed that I could find a safe method of disposing of you. I am actually to have a hundred pounds as soon as I can prove Stavanger's enemies to be no longer in the land of the living. Nice for you, isn't it? But there is no fear of my ever earning that hundred pounds, nor of him ever employing anyone else to earn it, since he is sure to be in your power soon."

XIII

MORE DISAPPOINTMENTS

The "Hornby Cross," having accomplished its voyage in safety, was viewed with considerable interest as it was being manœuvred into Millwall Dock, whither it had brought a cargo of grain from India. Among the onlookers were a few whose attention was the result of curiosity alone; but the greater part of the small crowd assembled at the dock gates had business of some sort on board. There were relatives and friends of the returning seafarers, eagerly looking out for their own folk, and anxious to see them again after their long voyage. And there were numbers of touters for nearly every trade that can be patronised by seafarers. There was also Mr. Gay, a detective whom we have met before, talking to an elderly clergyman and a slim young man, whose clear blue eyes keenly watched the operations on board the incoming vessel.

Presently she was near enough to be boarded by the most venturous spirits in the crowd, and these were soon clambering about in what seemed a very reckless fashion to those unused to the sight. Among the first to touch the "Hornby Cross's" deck was Mr. Gay, and he at once made for the captain, who was standing on the bridge, contentedly watching the operations of the dock pilot, into whose charge the vessel had been put.

"Good morning, sir," said Mr. Gay, touching his hat in greeting. "I am glad to see you safe in port. My name is Gay. You will have received the note I sent you by the pilot this morning."

"Your name is Gay, is it? Well, I guess you won't feel like your name for a bit. Your note came too late, sir."

"The deuce! Do you mean to say that Morton, as he calls himself, has given us the slip?"

"I do. You see, I would have done my best to help you if I had had only half a notion who my passenger was. As I hadn't, you can't be surprised at being done."

"But the man really started from Bombay with you?"

"Yes, he really did. But he didn't choose to come all the way with us, and I had no reason for supposing that he was wanted here. We had to call at Gibraltar for bunker coals, and Mr. Morton expressed a fancy to remain behind and explore Spain. I reckon he had funked about coming to England, and thought the Spaniards would be better chums with a rogue."

"My clients will be dreadfully disappointed. Everything seems to go against them."

"It seems to me that in this case it is your own stupidity that has gone against them. You must excuse the remark, but it expresses what I think."

"And in what way have I been stupid, may I ask?"

"Well, you might have found out where we were likely to bunker. The owners would have given you the information. Then you could have come out to intercept your man before he had a chance to clear, instead of waiting here expecting him to walk into the trap set for him. Or you could have cabled to me to detain him. But, of course, these little items are things a detective wouldn't be likely to think of."

"I feel quite grateful for your sympathy in my disappointment, Captain Criddle, but feel it necessary to correct you in a few particulars. Even though only a detective, I was struck with the idea that it would be wise to consult the owners. Their information left only the course adopted open to me. I was told that you had probably already taken in bunker coals at Malta, and that you would not be calling at any other place before your arrival in England. It is only six days since we learned that Morton, or, more correctly speaking, Stavanger, was on board your ship, and either meeting him, or cabling to have him detained was out of the question. You received instructions through the pilot at Gravesend, and I fail to see what further steps could have been taken for the man's capture, unless we had been more accurately informed of your proceedings by your owners."

"Oh, well, it isn't their fault, as they knew no different. But I haven't time to talk anymore, as I have a swarm of people to see. Good afternoon."

Thus peremptorily dismissed, Mr. Gay found it necessary to return to shore without the prize he had hoped to land with him, and his professional chagrin was mingled with real sorrow for the bitter disappointment of his clients. He was not a little angry with Captain Criddle for his want of sympathy and his unflattering insinuations. These were, no doubt, prompted by the reluctance felt by most people to have anything to do with a criminal case in any shape or form, and Detective Gay was not far wrong when he suspected Captain Criddle of being rather pleased than otherwise that the expected arrest had not taken place on board his ship.

That the Corys were deeply dismayed is a foregone conclusion, and that Mr. Cory thought it useless to make further investigations for a while is not surprising.

"The man won't have stayed in Gibraltar, that is certain," he said. "And if we were to go there, and follow up the trail, it is doubtful if we could ever track him and secure his return to England. So long as he chooses to remain in Spain, so long is he safe. Even if he leaves there I'm afraid his pursuit would be but a wild goose chase. His predilection for aliases will make identification difficult, and he seems to possess some abnormal instinct that cautions him against coming danger."

"I think myself, sir," observed Mr. Gay, "that he won't come back to England, at all events, until he has run through his plunder. Even then he may be quietly supplied with money by his father, whom we believe to to be in league with him. If I were you I would not move in the matter for a while, in order to lull all suspicion of pursuit. If we can stumble on Captain Cochrane in the meantime, so much the better. We may be able to prove Mr. Riddell's innocence through him."

"And if we do not stumble on Captain Cochrane?" inquired Annie, whose assumption of masculine garb made it more imperative upon her to keep her composure than would have been the case had she been figuring simply as Annie Cory.

"In that case it will be difficult to bring conviction to the minds of judge and jury, if you decide to move for a fresh inquiry."

"But the ring which the present captain of the 'Merry Maid' is bringing home with him?"

"That may prove valuable evidence, or it may not, just as it happens."

"It is bound to be valuable evidence when it is identified as part of the stolen property, as it is sure to be."

"By whom?"

"By whom? Why, by the Stavanger Bros., or by Mr. Riddell, who inventoried the goods the night they disappeared."

"Well, I don't want to dishearten you too much; but I feel it my duty to show you how difficult the case really is. No doubt Mr. Riddell could recognise this diamond ring. But would his word be accepted? He was convicted of the robbery by overwhelming evidence, which it is now to his interest to negative by every means in his power. It is, therefore, natural that he should try to remove the onus of guilt from his own shoulders to that of another, by swearing to property traced to that other's possession. Pray, don't be angry! I am not stating a private conviction that Mr. Riddell would swear falsely, but that a chuckle-headed judge or jury would be likely to think so. When a man is once down, the world likes to keep him down."

"But," put in Mr. Cory, "there are the Brothers Stavanger, who would know the ring as well as Mr. Riddell, presumably better."

"And how are we to guarantee that they will aid the ends of justice by identifying that which will help to prove the son of the one and the nephew of the other to be a thief, a perjurer, and an absconding vagabond? The reputation of both the firm and the family depends upon Hugh Stavanger's safety. I firmly believe that they have already done some false swearing in the matter. Is it likely that they will reverse their former tactics and play into our hands now?"

"I'm afraid you are right. Still, we have several things to fall back upon that will help us, even if the evidence of the ring proves valueless."

"It cannot prove valueless," said Annie now, with considerable decision. "Captain Gerard will relate how he became possessed of it, and there is his letter to us by way of corroboration of his evidence. The Maltese jeweller will also help us, if necessary. So, even if we cannot bring the real culprits up for judgment, we can move for a new trial, and even if judge and jurors are as addlepated and obstinate as you would have us to believe, they must see that the case is much deeper and more complicated than they supposed. And if it is their natural propensity to doubt the word of people accused of crime, they will be as likely to exercise it upon the man now accused. Mr. Peary, our solicitor, must push things on without delay, and we will rely upon such evidence as we can produce, if we can secure a new trial. Meanwhile, there is still time to do some active work, and a plan I have in my head may result in the discovery of a clue to Hugh Stavanger's whereabouts."

What that plan was Annie would not disclose, though pressed upon the point both by her father and the detective. The latter was very much annoyed at the turn events had taken, and was by no means sanguine as to the ultimate results of the investigations that were being pursued on Harley Riddell's behalf. But he went away with a higher admiration of Annie Cory's pluck than he had ever felt for that of any woman in his life.

"She is game to the core," he thought, "and if anybody can help the poor fellow in gaol, it is his sweetheart, who, it seems to me, cannot be daunted. She is one in a million. Most girls would have sat down and fretted, instead of trying to remedy the evil. Well, good luck to her, say I. If a girl like that doesn't deserve to succeed, nobody does."

From which remarks it may be gathered that Mr. Gay was not one of those who, to cover their discomfiture, would begrudge success to another, because he or she did not happen to be in the profession.

A few weeks later the "Merry Maid" was safely docked again, and Annie, accompanied by her father, and still figuring as Mr. Ernest Fraser, was sitting in the cabin of the steamer talking to Captain Gerard. They had awaited his arrival at the dock, being too impatient to stay at home until he had time to visit them.

His face lengthened considerably as he listened to the long account of disappointment and failure they had to give him.

"Well, I'm hanged if ever I knew anything like it," he said at last, in a tone of great vexation. "I thought everything was plain sailing, and never dreamt that Stavanger would alter his mind about coming on to England. You can't touch him in Spain, and for anything we know he may stick there. I wonder where Cochrane is. He must have taken the alarm, too."

"We hope to be able to help the case considerably by means of the ring you wrote to us about," observed Mr. Cory.

"Well, the imp of mischief seems to be at work," said the captain, emphasising his vexation by an oath. "Even the ring will be no use as evidence now. At Malta we coaled, coming home. There I met an old chum, who, like myself, was on his first voyage as master. I'm afraid we both jubilated till we were half seas over. I was cutting a dash with the diamond ring at the time. My friend offered to go on board my ship with me. As we were being rowed to the ship he noticed my ring, and made some remark about it. I pulled it off to show it to him. Whether it was his fault or mine I hardly know, but between us we let the ring drop into the water, with the result that it is lost beyond recovery."

XIV

An Accommodating Postman

A nnie, my child, don't you think you had better give up this vain chase? You are looking ill and worried. The case makes no real progress, in spite of all our exertions, and you are wearing your life away for nothing."

"For nothing, auntie? Is Harley's rescue nothing? I'm ashamed to hear you speak like that. It's a good thing Mrs. Riddell has not come downstairs yet. She would be astonished to find you turning traitor."

"I have heard some people say, my dear, that you have a real nasty temper when you like, and I am bound to admit that they are not far wrong, for your last sentence was thoroughly ill-natured. As you know, however, I am quite ready to make allowances, and I repeat that you are not reaping an equivalent success for all your exertions."

"And what would you have me do? Leave Harley to his fate, without another effort to save him?"

"By no means. I am as anxious as ever that he should be helped. But I think you will work more efficiently if you take things quietly for a while, and resume operations after your inactivity has lulled all suspicion."

"You mean well, auntie; but I should die if I didn't work in some way or other for Harley's benefit. So far all my efforts have failed, but I don't mean to give up hope, for Fate cannot always set her signals dead against us."

The above conversation between Miss Cory and her niece will serve to show that poor Harley Riddell, while possessing friends who were as firmly convinced of his innocence as ever, was in danger of having his prospects jeopardised by the paralysing influence of baffled efforts. Annie was the only one whom disappointment did not seem to daunt, and, with her, failure was but a stimulus to renewed effort. The long-drawn-out agony of her lover's unjustified incarceration was ever before her eyes, and she would have deemed herself guilty of a crime had she resigned herself to the passive inactivity which to others seemed the only course left her.

"Are you going out this morning?" questioned Miss Margaret, as she carefully examined a hole in the damask tablecloth she was about to darn.

"Yes. I have a little business to transact. Tell father I won't be long, for, if I am, I shall have been unexpectedly detained."

Presently our heroine, who to the ordinary passerby looked a rather handsome young fellow, with short, dark hair, bright dark blue eyes, and a dark moustache, of a shape which suited his light form and clearly-cut features to perfection, was walking down the street in a westerly direction at a rapid pace.

Half an hour later this same young gentleman was to be seen talking to an elderly postman, in a neighbourhood which, for the sake of the aforementioned postman I had better not indicate too closely. Suffice it to say that his round embraced the residence of Mr. David Stavanger, who, with his family, was now back in London.

"Have you anything yet for me?" was the first inquiry addressed to the postman, an inquiry, moreover, which pointed to a little previous collusion between the two innocent-looking individuals.

"I believe I have, at last, sir," was the answer, "I had an extra lot of letters this morning, and very near forgot all about you. In fact, I was just putting three letters in the letter-box of Number Thirty-nine when I caught sight of a foreign stamp, and stuck to the letter it was on, just in time. Is this anything in your line, sir?"

Saying this, the postman handed a letter to "Mr. Bootle," which the latter seized with avidity, and examined eagerly. The scrutiny appeared to more than satisfy him. He was positively jubilant, for the missive bore a Spanish postmark, and was in the handwriting which had become quite familiar to the pseudo governess of Fanny Stavanger.

"I believe this is the very thing I want. Wait a moment until I open it, so that I may know whether I need your services anymore for the present or not. There! you see there is no cheque or valuable paper of any description in this envelope. It is, as I told you, a letter only that I wished to intercept, and there will be no inquiry about it, I assure you, as the writer is a fugitive from justice, who is only too anxious to keep dark. Yes, this tells me all I want to know. This very night I set off to catch my man, and here is the ten-pound note I promised you."

"If you have gold about you it would suit me better, sir. Ten pounds is a lot for a poor chap like me to have, and folks might get suspicious if I showed a note for that amount."

"Perhaps you don't feel sure that the note is genuine. I have no gold with me. But if you object to the bank note, I will give you a cheque on the National and Provincial Bank."

"Oh, it's all right, sir. I'll take your word for it. All the same, if you don't mind, I'll follow you till we get to the bank. Then you can go inside with me, and change it."

It was evident that the postman distrusted him. But Mr. Bootle was too delighted with the prize he had obtained to be very thin-skinned about this stranger's opinion. In due time the postman received £10 in gold as payment for his breach of confidence, and went on his way rejoicing, wishing for a speedy opportunity of doing another such profitable day's work.

As for Mr. Ernest Bootle, he went on his way rejoicing, too, and feeling not the slightest qualm of conscience at what he had done, since it was all in the cause of right and justice. The precious letter was hugged very closely during the journey home, and then, in the privacy of Mr. Bootle's own room, it was re-read.

For the benefit of the reader we will transcribe its contents here:—

Lina, Spain

My Dear Father,

"I am still inclined to stop in this place for a while. Nobody has the slightest suspicion that I am not a *bonâ fide* English agent and that my name is not Gregory Staines. You still urge me to come home. I think your advice unwise, for I am sure that girl will leave no stone unturned to find me, and arrest would be very distasteful to me. I am very much better as I am. I live in comfort, have no tiresome business restrictions, and, so far, have won so much in an English gaming-house here that it has not been necessary to encroach on the money I have realised. You need not imagine that I am careless, or that I am courting recognition. Even if anyone who knew me was to come here, I am too well disguised to be identified, and even if identification were possible, it would be useless, as I am quite safe in Spanish territory. And I am not staying at an hotel either, but have taken lodgings in a quiet, respectable neighbourhood, with a good-looking young English widow, who seems inclined to be sweet on me. If I find that she has any money put by I may perhaps marry her, and settle down here. I don't care much for swell society, so, if I can be made comfortable when at home, and I do not run out of spending money abroad, I shan't need to grumble.

In any case, I mean to give England a wide berth while that confounded woman is knocking around. I wish she would break her neck."

"No, I won't break my neck," said the individual to whom this pious wish applied. "But I'm hoping, after all, to stop your gallop, Mr. Stavanger, since you have so kindly put your new address in this letter; and the good-looking widow must be cured of her folly, too. I daresay you do feel yourself tolerably safe, and you are evidently free from qualms of conscience also. The latter, no doubt, will make themselves felt when you are brought to book for your crimes. Then you will, no doubt, be a pattern of pious repentance, since the gist of repentance, in convicted criminals, is to be measured by the poignancy of their regret at being found out. The exceptions to this rule are the very, very few who voluntarily own their culpability and surrender themselves to justice. As you are not likely to prove a voluntary repentant, I must force your hand. And now for my immediate plans."

The result of the deliberations in which Mr. Bootle now indulged will be apparent in a letter which the Rev. Alexander Bootle, otherwise Mr. Cory, read up to his sister, and to Mrs. Riddell the same evening. Said letter merely informed them that Annie was now gone to carry out the plan at which she had hinted some days ago; that she was sanguine of success; that she wished her departure from home kept as quiet as possible; that she had, according to an understanding between them, drawn as much money as she thought might be needed for the enterprise she had in hand; and that they must not feel uneasy if they did not hear from her for sometime, as she did not wish to risk the failure of her enterprise by allowing even her nearest and dearest to know of her whereabouts.

"I hope Annie will not plunge into any foolish risks," said Miss Margaret, anxiously.

"She is too sensible to do that," Mrs. Riddell remarked. "Still, she has courage surpassing that of 99 out of every 100 women, and would think little of what would scare others."

"And her very pluck will carry her safely through dangers that another woman would succumb to. I think Harley is lucky in having won so devoted a girl. For she will never relax her efforts, and I begin to be imbued with her faith in ultimate success."

"So do I," added Mr. Cory. "All the same, I wish she had taken us into her confidence. The child is only twenty, and has never been entirely thrown on her own resources before. Suppose she were to fall into the hands of swindlers, and be robbed of the money she has with her? All sorts of evils might happen before she could communicate with us."

"John, I'm surprised at you. Annie is too much in earnest, and at the same time too wary, to play into the hands of the enemy. You don't like the notion of her pursuing her investigations alone. After all, it is the best thing she can do; for you must admit that neither you nor the detective have been much use in the case."

"That was due to adverse circumstances, not to our want of penetration."

"I am willing to grant that; but I have no doubt that Annie is actuated by an idea that she is less likely to put Stavanger on his guard if alone than if accompanied by anyone else. For my part I have resolved not to be uneasy about her. Have you heard anything of what the Stavangers are doing just now?"

"Jogtrotting, as per usual, I suppose, except that the elder daughter is to be married soon. I am not sure that it is not today."

"I'm sorry for the man who marries into that family. But, of course, we have no grounds for warning him. And now about Harley. It is wonderful how he keeps his health. Oh, are you going to bed, Mrs. Riddell? Well, goodnight. Perhaps all is going to be cleared up soon, and you must keep your spirits up, for your son's sake."

"For the sake of my sons, yes," said the old lady tremulously. "And for the sake of the dear girl who has done so much for them and for me."

"Strange how the dear old soul clings to that belief in Hilton's ultimate recovery," said Miss Margaret, when she and her brother were once alone. "Nothing seems to convince her that he is really dead."

"We have plenty of proof that he is dead. There is the word of all the people who voyaged with him in the 'Merry Maid' that he disappeared in mid-ocean. And the length of time that has now elapsed precludes all possibility of his being alive still."

"Of course, he must be dead. And our poor friend will be bound to awaken in time to the bitter truth that the sea will not give up its dead."

"If you please," announced a servant, whose knock had not been heard by the brother and sister, "a gentleman, whose name is Captain Gerard, wishes to speak to you."

"Gerard! Show him in at once. Perhaps he has some important news for us, Margaret."

ELIZABETH BURGOYNE CORBETT

"We'll hope so. And we shall soon know."

"Good evening, Mr. Bootle," said Captain Gerard, advancing into the room. "You will, perhaps, be surprised to receive a visit from me so late in the day. But the truth is I have a bit of news for you that may interest you—I have seen Captain Cochrane."

XV

Just in Time

We will now, with the reader's permission, retrace our history to the night on which the captain and passenger of the "Merry Maid" consigned to the waves the body of the man whom they firmly believed to have murdered.

The barque "Halcyon," bound from Lisbon for Callao, was proceeding quietly on her course and had, up to now, encountered nothing out of her usual experience. The captain, contentedly smoking a big cigar, was leaning idly over the rail and scanning the horizon, on the faint chance of seeing something that would relieve the monotony of the scene. It was a fine moonlight night, but now and again a cloud, carried along a higher strata than that by which the movements of the "Halcyon" were dominated, obscured the radiance of the orb of night, and enveloped sea and sky in a temporary mantle of darkness, rendering invisible everything but the distant lights of some vessel crossing the track pursued by the "Halcyon." Captain Quaco Pereiro, being of an adventurous disposition, would have preferred more variety in the scenery. But he was withal of a philosophical turn of mind, and never fretted for that which was unobtainable. Being content, therefore, to accept his somewhat isolated position uncomplainingly, he was nevertheless prepared to welcome relief in any form, and followed with considerable interest the course of a steamer, of which he obtained an occasional feeble glimpse, and which he concluded, from the track pursued, to be bound for the Mediterranean. Not that there was anything special about the steamer to attract his attention. But it chanced to be the nearest object in sight, therefore possibly the most profitable to observe.

But nothing occurred on board that he was near enough to distinguish, and Captain Pereiro, having finished his cigar, and having bethought himself that it would be as well to go below for a drink of wine, was raising himself up from the rail against which he had been leaning, when his eyes caught sight of a dark object bobbing quietly about on the waters, offering no resistance beyond that inert resistance which is inherent in any solid substance.

"H'm! what is that?" he questioned himself. "A log of wood? Yes—no—ah! Sancta Maria! it is the body of a man! Holy Mother, preserve us!"

Such a sight always saddened Captain Pereiro, for it reminded him of what might possibly be his own fate, and made him pray the more fervently that the beloved wife and children whom he had left at home might be long ere they were deprived of their bread winner. Imagining that it was the body of some shipwrecked sailor that was now within a boat's length of him, he was about to turn away from the painful sight, when his heart gave a startled bound on hearing a weird cry, as of some human being in the depths of agony and despair.

"Mother of God!" he cried, crossing himself vigorously, "what was that?"

Convinced that the cry he had heard did not originate on board, Captain Pereiro turned his gaze over the side again in the direction of the weird object which had already impressed him painfully. With ears and eyes strained to their utmost tension, he waited for he scarcely knew what. Would the body float quietly past, with not a sign of life or vitality about it? Or would his impressions be realised, and would it turn out that the awful scream he had heard proceeded from that which he had shudderingly looked upon as a corpse?

He was not left many seconds to conjecture, for once more the moonlit air was rent with the desponding shriek of the dying, and this time all doubt and superstitious fear were simultaneously removed from his mind. For not only was it evident whence the cry proceeded, but the hands of the supposed corpse were thrown up imploringly, yet feebly, as though by one from whom the vital spark had nearly fled.

Others had now also both seen and heard what was going on, and it scarcely needed Captain Pereiro's sharp command to back the mainyard in order to induce his sailors to bring about the end he desired. In an incredibly short space of time the course of the "Halcyon" was arrested, a boat was lowered, the drowning man secured, and preparations for starting again made. As soon as rescuers and rescued were safely on board, Captain Pereiro gave the order to brace the mainyard, and speedily, with well-filled sails, the barque was being steered on her course once more.

It seemed, however, that the fine fellows had wasted their energies in a vain cause, for the stranger had relapsed into total unconsciousness, which was so profound that for a long time it resisted every benevolent effort to dispel it.

"The fates are against the poor fellow," murmured the captain, sorrowfully. "I fear we were too late to help him. And yet it is a shame to be so cheated after all the trouble. Pedro, we will have another try, and by the Virgin, I will renounce—I mean I will be angry with—my patron saint if he does not help us to succeed in keeping this man's soul out of purgatory a while longer."

Pedro, who, by the way, was the steward of the "Halcyon," was already fatigued by the vigorous exertions he had made. He was, moreover, convinced that the thing upon which he had been operating no longer contained a soul, and he felt a horror at the idea of pulling and twisting a dead body about. But he dared not refuse to do as he was told, so, invoking the aid of St. Peter as a corollary to the help St. George had been asked to extend to the captain, he set bravely to work once more, and soon became as full of faith and energy as Pereiro himself.

Fortunately for St. George, the captain had no need to be angry with him, for after a prolonged and fatiguing spell of rubbing, fomenting, dosing, and artificial respiration, the stranger's eyelids began to quiver, and short, gasping sighs escaped his labouring breast. Thanks to Pereiro's clever treatment, he was already partially relieved of the brine which he had perforce swallowed, but no sooner did the latter realise that his efforts were being rewarded by success, than he promptly administered another emetic, which proved thoroughly effectual, and left the patient gasping with exhaustion, but on the high road to recovery.

As the reader no doubt guesses, it was Hilton Riddell who was thus miraculously saved from what appeared to be certain death. His would-be murderers were so anxious to avoid observation on their own ship that they had not noticed the proximity of the barque at right angles with them, and felt as sure that they had compassed their desired end, as that they themselves were alive and well.

Thus they sped on their course, hugging the belief that they had taken the most effectual means of silencing an enemy, and feeling secure in the reflection that, as the sea was not likely to give up its dead, they were not likely to be confronted with Hilton Riddell again.

Meanwhile the latter was receiving every care and attention on board the "Halcyon." Captain Pereiro was greatly delighted to observe the gradual recovery of the prey he had rescued from the ocean, all the more so as he had already convinced himself that Hilton had been the victim of foul play. The blow on the head had been a terrible one—so terrible, indeed, that it threatened to kill him, many symptoms of concussion of the brain showing themselves. Thus it was weeks before poor Hilton recovered his wonted vigour, and, under God, it was due to the unremitting care and attention with which Captain Pereiro nursed him that he was enabled to evade death. Pedro, too, being of a generous disposition, grudged no pains in the preparation of dainties likely to stimulate the invalid's for sometime languishing appetite. Had Hilton been their patron saint himself, he could not have been treated with more care and tenderness, and his returning consciousness of what he had been saved from invested them, in turn, with every saint-like attribute.

Short, stout, of stolid feature; black-haired, rough-bearded, and carelessly shaven; with dark eyes, whose kindly light was almost obscured by bushy, overhanging eyebrows; of the swarthiest complexion; with big, coarse hands, and a rough gait, and with all the eccentricities of his appearance accentuated by a sublime indifference to the advantages of becoming attire, Captain Pereiro was not one to strike the casual observer with enthusiastic admiration. The steward, Pedro, did not come in a bad second as far as personal appearance went, except that he was taller, thinner, and more pronouncedly ungainly. But ask Hilton Riddell to this day to name the two finest fellows on earth, and he will at once utter a verdict in favour of the captain and steward of the Portuguese barque "Halcyon."

It was at first a source of wonderment to his rescuers how he had kept afloat so long, until they discovered that much of his apparent bulk was caused by a life-saving waistcoat with which he had had the forethought to provide himself.

"This man is English, and he comes from London. So much I can make out from his speech, but no more," said the captain, when talking things over with the mate of his ship, who, though not taking an active part in the nursing of the foundling, yet felt a considerable interest in his progress towards recovery. "He is a beautiful man, as beautiful as the fabled gods must have been; but I burn with curiosity to know how he has been thrown on to our hands. He has met with foul play, that is sure, and he has been among people whom he knew to be his enemies. That is also sure. It is also evident that he was to some extent prepared for the risk he ran, and that his enemies were ignorant of the fact. Otherwise he would not have worn this waistcoat, ready for inflation, under his shirt, or his enemies, after thinking they had killed him by the blows on the head, would have removed the wonderful garment which ensured his floating on the surface of the water."

"But," objected the mate, "he may have been wrecked, and the wound on his head may have been caused by a blow from floating wreckage."

"No, that is not so, for when I took a marlingspike, and pretended to hit my own head with it, at the same time pointing to his, he nodded vigorously, as much as to say that his wound was inflicted purposely. I am sure he has a strange history, and, for the first time in my life, I wish I knew how to talk English."

"If he could talk Portuguese it would do just as well."

"Yes; but he doesn't talk Portuguese, so there's an end of it. I will go below again now, and see how he is getting on."

Captain Pereiro found his patient very much better, and anxious to know where he was, how he came there, and whither he was being taken. But his eager questions, and the captain's willing answers, only resulted in their becoming more hopelessly befogged with each other. Neither could elicit or communicate anything satisfactory. At last the captain was seized with a bright idea, which induced him to rush to the chart-room as quickly as his unwieldy body would let him, leaving Hilton wondering what was the matter with him. Presently he returned with a triumphant look on his face, bearing in his hands a large roll, which he laid carefully on the locker for a while. Then he assisted Hilton into a sitting position, piling behind him a pair of sea boots, some oilskins, a camp stool, and sundry other things, upon which substantial foundation he arranged various pillows in the dexterous manner which had become habitual to him. Having thus made the patient as comfortable as possible, he produced the roll from the top of the locker and unfolded what proved to be a large chart.

Hilton smiled his sudden comprehension, and eagerly bent his eyes upon the chart. The captain, seeing that his purpose was likely to be understood, pointed first to Hilton, then to the chart, in effect asking him to give as much information as he could. Very soon Hilton put his finger on London and looked at the captain, who nodded comprehension. Then he slowly traced the course of the "Merry Maid" on the chart until nearly abreast Lisbon, when he stopped, feigned to go to sleep; to strike his head with his eyes shut; to awake struggling in the water; to withdraw a tube from his waistcoat pocket; and to inflate by its means a concealed life-saving garment. The captain thoroughly understood this pantomime, and clenched his fist in anger at those who had perpetrated so dastardly a deed. Then, once more pointing questioningly to the chart, he gave Hilton to understand that he wished to know whither the "Merry Maid" was bound, whereupon the remainder of the route to Malta was traced out for him. After this, being mutely questioned in his turn, Pereiro made a start at Lisbon, Hilton following his movements with breathless attention. Stopping near the spot indicated by the latter, he gave a sharp cry, tossed his arms as if struggling in the water, made a pantomimic rescue, and then began to rub himself vigorously, and to pump his arms up and down to show that artificial respiration had been resorted to. Hilton squeezed his hands gratefully, and murmured words of thanks, of which Pereiro had no difficulty in grasping the import, although they were uttered in a tongue of which he knew nothing but that it was English. After this, anxiously watched, he slowly traced a course which filled Hilton's heart with dismay, for he never stopped until he had rounded Cape Horn, and followed what seemed to his companion to be an interminable coastline.

Finally, he stopped at Callao, and was astounded to see that his information was received with every symptom of distress. For a time, Hilton knew not what to do, for he felt stunned. To go all that distance, and in a sailing vessel, too, was equivalent to being dead to friends and foes alike for many months. Moreover, he was rendered utterly useless, and could do nothing but fret and worry at the trouble which would be felt at home on his own account.

"My mother will wonder why she does not hear from me. Those scoundrels will forge some plausible tale to account for my disappearance, and poor Harley will be doomed to undergo the whole of his horrible sentence in prison, if, indeed, he lives so long. Between grief for Harley, and grief for me, my poor mother will fret herself into the grave. And poor Annie! My God! how everything is playing into the hands of those villains! It seems unbelievable—and there is that bottle of papers I threw overboard, too. Perhaps that will soon disclose the true state of affairs, and Harley's liberation may be effected without any further help from me."

Could he have foreseen the fate of the papers he had prepared so carefully, his distress of mind would have been much greater than it was. Fortunately, this knowledge was denied him, but he already suffered enough to cause him to have a relapse, and for sometime his condition gave great anxiety to his nurses.

After many days he was sufficiently convalescent to come on deck, and after that his physical progress was rapid. As he recovered his wonted strength and vigour, the admiration of those around him increased considerably. Some of them—indeed, all—used as they were to swarthy skins, and dusky locks, looked upon his smart, upright physique, his clear, fair skin, just relieved from effeminacy by being slightly tanned, his finely-cut features, his wavy, flaxen hair, his expressive grey eyes, and his small hands and feet, as the perfection of all that was gallant and beautiful in man. By-and-bye they also began to admire him for other than his physical qualities. For he was not disposed to be the idle and ungrateful recipient of bounty, but lost no opportunity of doing a service to his deliverers.

Ships are never overmanned. There is always room for the help of another hand or two. And even then, in squally weather, it taxes everybody's energies to keep pace with the exigencies of the hour. Thus, it often happened that Hilton proved himself invaluable, and though Captain Pereiro, with whom he was fast learning to converse in broken Portuguese, remonstrated with him for working so hard, he could not renounce any part of the active life he was now leading. For it served to save him from the despondency which he could not otherwise have resisted.

Nevertheless, he counted the months, the weeks, the days that must elapse ere he could obtain any news of what was transpiring at home, and every spell of adverse weather caused him acute anguish, since it lengthened the time during which he would have to remain inactive. But as all things come to those that wait, even so did the last day of his voyage dawn on Hilton Riddell, and it was with curiously mingled emotions that he once more found himself ashore. True, it was in a strange country, among a strange people, and thousands of miles away from the place in which he was anxious to find himself.

But it was, at any rate, a civilised country, to which English news might penetrate, and he was not without a faint hope that he might come across an English paper containing some account of progress made on Harley's behalf. How fallacious this hope was will be apparent to the reader, but one has to picture oneself in his destitute, lonely, and desperate condition, to realise to what mere straws of comfort one can cling for consolation. The "Halcyon" would be some weeks before it would be ready to leave Callao, and Captain Pereiro, who by this time knew a great deal of the Englishman's story, very generously urged him to make it his home until he could get himself transported back to England.

Being without money, and possessing no credit with anyone here, Hilton took the only course open to him under the circumstances, unless he had been willing to seek work, and remain here long enough to save money for his passage. This he could not do, as he deemed his speedy presence in England imperative, in Harley's interests. He therefore went to the British Consul, and represented himself as a seafarer, who had been washed overboard in a squall. His reason for being thus uncommunicative concerning what really occurred was that he feared that any report should reach England through the Consulate, and find its way into the English papers before he could arrive himself. He was fully alive to the fact that news of his safety would be gladly welcomed by his mother and friends. But he also knew that if his enemies were to suspect him to be in the land of the living, they would be on their guard, and would, perhaps, succeed once more in baulking him of the prey he meant to run to earth, in spite of what appeared to be a malignantly adverse fate.

"The bitterness of my loss is past," he said. "My people already mourn me dead, and my enemies triumph over my removal from their path. I will awaken neither the hopes of the one nor the fears of the other until the right moment for striking arrives. My blow will then be more deadly and sure, and I shall be able to work with much more freedom if my continued existence is unsuspected."

It was in conformity with this resolution that he gave fictitious names to the consul, both of himself and the ship from which he was supposed to have been washed overboard. Had there been much doubt expressed concerning the matter, there was the evidence of Captain Pereiro and his crew to show how he had come aboard the "Halcyon." Asked what he wished the consul to do for him, he replied that he was anxious to reach England as soon as possible; that, if chance afforded, he would gladly work his passage home; otherwise, he wished to be shipped free of charge to himself, on board a London-bound steamer, this request being in strict accordance with English usage and custom.

His request was looked upon as reasonable enough, and, upon the whole, he was well treated. But there was no vessel in the port that was likely to proceed to England immediately, and he was forced to submit to a heart-breaking delay. By this time Pereiro was very much attached to him, and would fain have persuaded him to wait until the "Halcyon" had discharged her cargo and reloaded, in order to return in the barque to Lisbon, thence to proceed by the quickest route to London.

"One of my sailors has asked me to let him off articles. He has come across a chance of making money more quickly than would be the case at sea. You can ship in his place, earn his pay, and have money to buy some clothes, and take you home to London. You will also be more at home with us than on another strange ship. Say the word, my friend, and make me happy."

But to this plan Hilton did not feel himself able to consent. The idea of another long voyage in a sailing vessel filled him with horror. Yet, as the weeks sped by, and no better opportunity offered itself, his hopes sank to zero. At last, when he was feeling thoroughly weary and despondent, another steamer bearing the English flag steamed into the harbour. This was the "Lorna Doone." Both officers and crew bore evidence of having undergone great privations, and the story they had to tell was enough to make anybody's heart ache. Head winds and heavy seas had delayed their outward passage, and sickness, in the shape of yellow fever, had overtaken them at their discharging port. All in turn had been seriously ill. Some of their shipmates had never recovered from the grip of Yellow Jack. Water, provisions, and men were alike scarce, and the captain, being in dire straits, had found it necessary to run into Callao for relief, before proceeding on the return voyage to Liverpool.

In all this Hilton hailed his opportunity. No sooner was the quarantine flag hauled down, than he boarded the "Lorna Doone," and asked to be shipped as an able seaman. Too sorely pushed to insist upon discharges or references, the captain gladly engaged him, and in another day or two the Blue Peter was flying on the foremast head of his new home.

It was with some regret, and many manifestations of sorrow, that the parting between Hilton and his demonstrative benefactors took place. But at last the painful scene was over; he was fairly installed on board the "Lorna Doone," and in a few hours more was being borne to the goal he was so anxious to reach—England.

XVI

A DETERMINED PURSUIT

In a certain house, in a certain street, in the town of Lina, Mrs. Dollman, a very pretty widow, of small attainments as far as time goes, for she was but 22, was talking to her sister, who had come to take tea with her. Said sister's name was Mrs. Twiley, and she lived at Gibraltar when at home, her husband being a sergeant-major there. The late Mr. Dollman had been a lieutenant stationed at the fortress. He had risen from the ranks by merit alone, and had nothing to live upon but his pay. When he died, with startling suddenness, his young wife found herself rather badly off, her widow's pension not leaving much margin for luxuries, after a certain number of necessities had been purchased.

Of relatives she had none left but the sister who lived in Gibraltar, and to whom she was much attached. She, therefore, resolved upon remaining in the vicinity, instead of going to England, where she knew very few people. A little kindly co-operation on the part of her late husband's friends enabled her to start a boarding-house on a small scale, with a view to supplementing her meagre income, and she was considered to be doing very well. Among her boarders was Hugh Stavanger, who was known here as Gregory Staines, and who was supposed to be a commission agent of some sort. Mr. Staines had been rather profuse in his attentions to his pretty landlady, and Mrs. Twiley, having heard something about a whispered possible engagement, deemed it compatible with her position as sole and serious relative to warn her sister against want of caution.

"You see, Phœbe," she said gravely, "you really know next to nothing about this Mr. Staines. Certainly, he seems to have plenty of money to go on with, and pays you regularly. But you want more than that. You want to feel that his past life will bear investigation, and that he is really actuated by no mercenary motives in seeking to marry you."

"Why, good gracious, Millie! I haven't a penny saved up, as you know; and, as for my pension, I shall forfeit that if I marry again. So how can anybody possibly want to marry me through mercenary motives?"

"Will often says that with all your native shrewdness, there are some points on which you are awfully slow, and I am inclined to agree with him. Do you forget that you have a very well-furnished house, with every article in it paid for; that you have a comfortable little business nicely established; and that you are such a capital little manager that many an adventurer would jump at the chance of being kept by you? Now, don't lose yourself in a temper, for I don't mean to insinuate that you couldn't be loved for yourself, apart from the material advantages you have to offer. In fact, I know different, for Archer Pallister thinks and dreams of nothing but your looks and ways, and I am sure that if he isn't downright genuine, there isn't a genuine man on earth. Indeed, the woman who marries him may thank her lucky stars. But there are all sorts of people knocking around, and Will says that we ought to be on our guard against Englishmen dodging about in Spain, unless they can give a very satisfactory account of themselves. For anything we know, this Gregory Staines is either an absconding building society secretary, or a fraudulent poor-rate collector."

"I think it's real mean of you to talk like that, Millie. You ought to know me better than to think I would take up with an adventurer."

"I am glad to hear you say so, my dear. Will, too, will be highly pleased to be told that you are going to give Mr. Staines the cold shoulder."

"You are rather premature. I never said so."

"Not in so many words, perhaps. But you implied it. You said that you wouldn't take up with an adventurer."

"Your conclusion does not follow."

"Indeed it does, dear, for I firmly believe the man to be a worthless adventurer."

"He is a jeweller's agent, doing a good business."

"So he says. But haven't you noticed that he transacts his business at very unbusiness-like times? He's out today, but the circumstance is exceptional. He generally goes to bed about two o'clock, rises late, loafs about the house for hours, and goes out upon this ostensible business of his towards evening, when work of his sort is, or ought to be, over. Besides, how could an agent live by doing business in Lina alone? Will and I are not the only two people who have talked him over, and the consensus of opinion is that he is not to be trusted, and is a man against whom you ought to be warned."

"It is very kind of you to talk about my private affairs to all sorts of people. Be good enough to tell Will that I'm exceedingly obliged to him."

"Now, don't be rusty! You know that Will is as fond of you as I am, and that nothing would grieve him more than to think you were unhappy. Oh, look what a pretty girl is getting out of that conveyance! Why, she is coming here. I wonder what she wants."

Phœbe Dollman also forgot her slight illhumour, and looked with interest upon the tall golden-haired beauty approaching the door. Presently a card was brought in to Mrs. Dollman, and the Spanish servant informed her that a lady wished to speak to her. The name on the card was Una Stratton, and very speedily Mrs. Dollman was conversing with the owner of it.

Miss Stratton, it appeared, was a lady artist, who wished to enrich her portfolio by sketching some Spanish scenes and people. She had been recommended to Mrs. Dollman's boarding-house by a Mr. Smith, who had obtained the address for her from a friend who had spent a few weeks at Lina in the early summer.

Mrs. Dollman did not know who could be the especial gentleman who had been good enough to recommend her lodgings. But she had had several boarders who were little more than birds of passage, being en route for other places, and the gentleman through whom Miss Stratton had obtained her address might be one of those. Anyhow, things seemed to be straightforward enough. The young lady offered to pay for her board in advance, and Mrs. Dollman, who was quite charmed with the new arrival, promptly closed with her. Nor did she raise any objections when Miss Stratton announced that she wished to bring another boarder with her in the shape of a big Newfoundland dog, who was even now waiting outside for her.

In a very short time everything was satisfactorily arranged, and the new boarder installed in comfortable quarters.

"This is my sister, Mrs. Twiley," said Mrs. Dollman sometime later. "She and her husband are my only relatives, and whoever knows me, speedily knows them, for they are good enough to spend a great deal of time with me."

"Your sister! You make me feel quite envious. I have neither sister nor brother, and have often felt rather lonely in consequence."

"But you have other relatives?"

"Oh, yes! I have the best father in the world. And my aunt—God bless her!—has been the most tender and affectionate of mothers to me."

"Then, after all, you ought to be happy, in our opinion, for it has always seemed to us that young people without a parental home are the most to be commiserated."

"And yet, with every possible advantage of home and family, one may be overtaken by troubles beside which the mere death of a loved one is comparative happiness."

As the beautiful stranger uttered the last words, her eyes darkened with grief, and her whole appearance betokened the most bitter sorrow. Both Millie and Phœbe were stricken with sudden awe before this brief glimpse of an anguish which evidently surpassed anything they had ever dreamed of, and their hearts went out tenderly towards Miss Stratton. Very quickly, however, the latter regained control of herself, and five minutes later the sisters were ready to doubt whether she was not one of the happiest of mortals.

"Have you any boarders in the house, Mrs. Dollman?" she inquired presently, while occupied in despatching the refreshing meal which had been promptly ordered for her. As she waited for a reply she toyed with her teaspoon, patted her big dog on the head, and altogether looked so carelessly unconcerned, that much more suspicious people than those she had to deal with would have been slow to fancy that her question was one of vital import to her, or that she was listening for the reply with every nerve tingling with anxiety.

"Only four," was Phœbe's answer. "We have a Mr. Everton and his wife. They have been here six months, and are likely to remain here. Then there are two single gentlemen, Mr. Grice and Mr. Staines."

Miss Stratton's heart leapt at this answer, yet she received it with apparent indifference, although it relieved her of a great anxiety. Suppose Mr. Gregory Staines, whose presence here was really her sole reason for coming to Lina, had suddenly taken it into his head to seek fresh quarters! She did not doubt her ability to trace him again. But each delay that occurred before running the man to earth prolonged the sufferings of the man whose liberty she had sworn to secure, and she was thankful to have found him at last.

Contrary to Phœbe's expectation, she betrayed not the slightest further interest in the other lodgers, but conversed for awhile pleasantly on other topics, inquiring carefully about the neighbouring scenery under the pretence of being anxious to take some local views.

"My artistic work is not necessarily bread and butter to me," she observed. "But I naturally wish to do as well as possible while I am here, as they may not be willing to spare me from home long."

"I would like to see your sketches, if you don't mind showing them to us," said Millie.

"And you shall see them," was the answer. "But not this evening. I suppose my box will be here soon, but by the time I have unpacked what is necessary, I shall be ready to go to bed, for I am very tired with travelling."

And this excuse, although not quite in accordance with Una Stratton's ultimate intentions, served to secure her the privacy she desired for the rest of the evening. She had casually learned that the other boarders were out, and that they were not likely to put in an appearance until sometime later.

"Mr. and Mrs. Everton are spending the day with some friends in Gibraltar. Mr. Grice never comes in until eight o'clock, and Mr. Staines' movements are so uncertain that we never know whether he will be in to supper or not. We generally have it soon after eight, and spend the rest of the evening at cards or music. We shall be very glad of your company. But are you quite sure that you will like the room you have chosen? As a rule, ladies do not feel so safe in a bedroom on the ground floor, and I have a chamber on the third floor, quite as pretty, if you would prefer it."

But to this suggestion Una, as we will at present call the girl in whom the reader has already recognised Annie Cory, returned a negative answer, saying that she preferred not to take her dog up and down the stairs. "He always sleeps in my room," she added, "and is such a splendid protector that I could not possibly feel nervous with him near me. I could not answer for his carefulness with the stair carpets, and always prefer to keep him to the ground floor."

This sounded plausible enough, and Millie remarked with a laugh that it would be a bold burglar who would dare to invade a room guarded by so powerful an animal.

"I think so too," said Una. "But he is as gentle as a lamb, unless bidden to be otherwise, and I am sure you will like him. Eh, Briny? You are a dear old thing, aren't you?"

Briny acknowledged the compliment by a stately wave of his tail, and by gently inserting his nose in the hand of his mistress, knowing that she always had a caress to spare for him.

Soon after Miss Stratton had retired with her dog to her own room, Millie's husband came to see his sister-in-law, and to escort his wife home to their quarters. The new arrival was liberally discussed and enthusiastically praised. But Sergeant-Major Twiley was disposed to receive all praises of the beautiful stranger *cum grano salis*, and rather hurt the feelings of his women-folks by offering to go round to a certain English hotelkeeper to have a look at the London directory, which served as a sort of guarantee to the *bona fides* of would-be creditors. He found nothing, however, but a substantiation of the new lodger's statements. The name and address she had given both tallied with those in the directory. So Sergeant-Major Twiley was reassured, and the ladies found their convictions confirmed.

But what would the three of them have thought if they could have seen what was now going on in the room to which the supposed Miss Stratton had retired, avowedly with the object of securing a goodnight's rest?

XVII

Running Him Down

Now, Briny," said Miss Stratton, having assured herself that there was no possibility of her either being overseen or overheard, "we shall have to be smart lest we startle our game too soon again. I think that with all his attempts at disguise it will take him all his time to deceive me. I wonder what he will think of me when he comes under the spell of the fascinations I mean to exercise over him? H'm! Perhaps he is not very susceptible, and won't be fascinated. In that case, I mean to work upon another tack. I only hope that I have studied the art of make-up sufficiently to prevent me from committing a hopeless blunder. Madame D'Alterre charged plenty for her instructions, and, so far, I am doing credit to them."

As Miss Stratton talked to her dog, she patted and caressed him, and altogether treated him as if he could understand every word she said. For his part, he made no noisy demonstrations of approval, but showed his sympathy and appreciation in his own dignified way. Then he laid himself beside the door and watched the transformation which his mistress soon began to make in her appearance. Truth to say, the change effected was sufficiently startling to deceive even the keenest observer, and perhaps Briny himself would have been at fault if he had not been already initiated into some of his owner's curious habits.

In about an hour Miss Stratton was nowhere to be seen, and in her place stood the young gentleman who has been introduced to the reader as Mr. Bootle. Enjoining the dog to remain at his post, Mr. Bootle put the light out, after placing some matches ready for use. Then he raised the blind and looked out of the window. Greatly to his delight, it proved to be a French window, opening into the garden, which was now dark and deserted, but from which it was easy to emerge unobserved into a lane which communicated with the main street. Before leaving the garden, however, after closing the window, Mr. Bootle reconnoitred a little, for he had an idea that Mrs. Dollman's dining-room had a window which overlooked this part of the premises. The supposition proved quite correct, and what was equally important was the fact that the window was not too closely blinded. As it did not present any points of observation for the ordinary passerby, particular care was not deemed necessary.

Regulating his movements with all possible care, Mr. Bootle contrived to obtain a good view of the persons seated round the table, occupied in partaking of supper. Sergt.-Major Twiley and his wife were there, and there were two other gentlemen present. The sergeant-major was easy to distinguish, and it took Mr. Bootle but a very short time to decide which of the other two men was the one posing as Mr. Gregory Staines, for one of them was a podgy, red-faced man, with clear, honest blue eyes, that would certainly have been very much out of place on his vis-à-vis's face.

"There now, Mr. S., I have got a good look at you unobserved," was the inward comment of the unseen watcher. "I must now take measures for keeping you under my notice without being suspected by you."

Five minutes later our friend, cigarette in hand, was promenading carelessly up and down the front street, and keeping a sharp look-out upon Mrs. Dollman's door. It was half-past nine when at last his vigil was rewarded by the sight he hoped for. Mr. Gregory Staines was bent upon either business or amusement, and was hurrying ahead of Mr. Bootle, perfectly unsuspicious of the fact that he was being followed. Lina is not a very large place, and it did not take long for either individual to reach the goal aimed at.

Mr. Bootle, otherwise Annie Cory, felt a slight accession of nervousness on entering the hotel to which Mr. Staines hurried as if he were afraid of missing some of the fun going on inside. But, although Annie found herself entering upon a totally new phase of life, she sauntered through the vestibule, and into a large saloon behind Staines, as if she were quite used to the habits of the society to which she was now being introduced. Following the example of her unconscious guide, she seated herself at a small table, and ordered a drink of brandy. Her reason for ordering brandy was soon apparent. While keenly taking note of all that transpired around her, she only feigned to drink, and after a while, watching her opportunity, she deftly substituted an empty glass for the one she was supposed to be using. In this way she fairly accounted for her presence in the place without appearing to be an unprofitable customer. Her next proceeding was to follow Mr. Staines into a side-room, in the centre of which stood a table, round which were seated some men playing at cards. The game was being watched by about a score of onlookers, and it was easy to stand among them and elude special observation. After about twenty minutes spent impatiently by

Mr. Staines, that gentleman found someone to play with him, and was forthwith transformed into a happy man, for his adversary, though not an inexperienced player, was too excitable to stand the smallest chance of beating such a combination of skill, coolness, and knavery as now confronted him. Mr. Staines, although his luck was almost miraculous, seemed to have as yet aroused no suspicions of unfair play. Now and again he lost a trifle, but Mr. Bootle concluded that these occasional losses were deliberately effected solely for the purpose of preserving the confidence and stimulating the gambling propensities of the people whose money the unscrupulous fellow meant to win.

"I think I will drop it," said Mr. Staines at last, putting his winnings into his pocket. "Luck seems all my way tonight, and I don't think it fair to go on playing, for I have no wish to skin anybody out."

But this show of consideration for others had precisely the effect anticipated by the speaker. The majority of his hearers were English, and they did not relish the imputation of unskilfulness thus adroitly thrown upon them.

"No, sir," said a tall, military-looking man, whose eyes were already bright between the excitement of play and the worship of Bacchus. "It is not good enough to excuse yourself in that way just when luck is on the point of turning. I demand my revenge, and these gentlemen will all agree that I am right, eh?"

There was an immediate chorus of approval from the onlookers to whom the speaker appealed.

"Yes, yes; give him his revenge," was the cry. "For my part," added a fast young subaltern, "I think it deuced mean to want to leave off at such a critical time."

"Nothing of the sort," shouted a half-tipsy individual, whose outward appearance gave very little indication of the nature of his profession or pursuits. "I consider that Mr. Staines has behaved like a man, and if anybody dares to say otherwise I'll knock him down."

The speaker looked big enough and brawny enough to imbue his hearers with the belief that he was quite able to carry out his threat. His utterances were therefore received with something like the respect they merited by all but the fast young sub. already mentioned.

"The proof of the pudding is in the eating," sneered he; "it will be easy for your friend to prove his fairness by accepting Captain Gale's challenge to continue playing, and if it comes to knocking people down, why, then, two can play at that game."

The altercation, although a mere interchange of empty boasts, struck Mr. Bootle as a very violent scene indeed, and it was a great relief when Mr. Staines soothingly spoke to the antagonists, thanking one for his straightforward championship, and assuring the other that he was ready either to play or to go home, just as seemed best to those whose money he had won.

"And," he added, "if the gentleman who has challenged me for his revenge doubts my fairness, I am ready to return him the money I have won, and to forego the pleasure of a friendly game with him in future."

"No, no," was the immediate verdict. "The money was won in fair play, and Captain Gale only wants his revenge."

So, presently, the game was resumed with increased zest, and small bets as to the results were indulged in, while glasses were emptied and replenished with a beautiful disregard of the probable effects of their contents upon the system. Mr. Bootle had made occasional feints of drinking, but could not help being amused to see how easy it was to substitute an empty glass for his own, without arousing the suspicions of those who profited by the change. The babel of voices, the frequent oaths, the tobacco-laden atmosphere, were all antagonistic to Mr. Bootle's ideas of comfort. But he, or rather she, would have braved much greater inconveniences than these, rather than forego the slightest chance of benefiting Harley.

So far, however, she had not made much progress. Her object was to scrape a casual acquaintance with Mr. Staines, from which she hoped to evolve events that would work in her favour. But the early morning hours arrived before the opportunity she sought was hers. Gregory Staines played steadily on—first with one player, and then with another; first losing, then winning a game, with apparently commendable impartiality. Perhaps he did not keep careful note of the money that changed hands with startling frequency. But there was no lack of keen observers present, who, perhaps stimulated by the insinuations of the antagonistic sub., noted the fact that Gregory Staines' winning games had almost invariably a greater amount at stake than the games at which he was the loser.

The latter, slightly carried away by his success, was losing his habitual caution, and was inclined to play as long as he could find anyone to play with him. Nor did he observe the angry scowls with which his triumphs were now being greeted by two or three of the men whom he had despoiled of their pocket money, until a warning hand was laid for a moment on his shoulder, and a voice whispered in his ear:—"Take care; you have enemies in the room."

Glancing swiftly round, he saw a slightly-built young fellow of medium height looking at him meaningly. His own glance betrayed some nervousness, for he never lost sight of the possibility of being tracked by the friends of Harley Riddell. But he was speedily reassured on that score, and looked upon this young stranger as a new arrival, who might, possibly, prove profitable to him.

"Enemies?" he inquired, in the same low tone used by the stranger. "What reason have you for supposing that I have enemies, either here or elsewhere?"

"Success always provokes enmity. You have been extraordinarily successful tonight. Losers generally imagine their losses due to anything but bad play, and I just now accidentally overheard something that is of importance to you."

"Another moment. Wait for me outside, if I am not asking too great a favour. I will follow you presently. Then we can discuss this matter more fully."

Annie was only too thankful to escape from the rank atmosphere, in which she felt almost choked, although she successfully managed to hide her discomfort from others. She was soon pacing about the front of the hotel, which was a frequent resort of Englishmen, and conducted very much upon the lines of an English institution of like status.

"Good heavens!" she muttered, "what am I made of that I can look at this man, and speak to him, without denouncing him to his face, and tearing from him the pitiful mask of respectability he still makes a show of wearing? Had I dreamt of all this a year ago, I could not have believed myself strong enough to show self-control like this. Ah! here he comes. I hope it will be easy to cultivate just the necessary amount of acquaintanceship with him. It will make my task easier, perhaps."

Shortly after this, Gregory Staines joined the individual who sauntered in the same direction, which chanced to be homewards for both of them, although the former little dreamed how closely his fate was linked with that of his companion. An earnest conversation now ensued, during which Mr. Staines was persuaded that certain words had been exchanged in the cardroom of the hotel, which promised anything but safety to him, in the event of his being caught out alone.

"And why should you interest yourself particularly in me?" he queried suspiciously, and received for answer, "Thereby hangs a tale, my dear sir.

I have an idea that you are, like myself, not too squeamish about trifles. Pray excuse me if I am mistaken. Perhaps I am not such a good judge of character as I fancy myself."

"That remains to be seen, Mr. Stranger. Anyhow, I'll see you at the same place tomorrow night again."

"Well, don't forget to be careful. Those scoundrels may have lost some of their animosity by tomorrow. Still, I have had an awkward scrape or two myself, and have no patience with thin-skinned fools, who have no business to play unless they can notch a point or two."

"But that wouldn't suit us."

"Perhaps not. Still, a certain gudgeon who is putting up at Gibraltar just now would be just in our line. I'll tell you all about him tomorrow. How far do you go in this direction?"

They were just opposite Mrs. Dollman's establishment as he spoke. But Mr. Bootle did not wish to appear too familiar with the ways of Mr. Staines at present. So he duly expressed his surprise on hearing that Mr. Staines was already at home. Then he bade him goodbye for the nonce, went round to the garden, and soon reached the room allotted to Miss Una Stratton, where he received a warm, but silent welcome from Briny, who had kept faithful vigil.

ELIZABETH BURGOYNE CORBETT

XVIII

A Wily Syren

When Una Stratton made her appearance next morning at breakfast she bore no evidence of having been up half the night, and her brilliant hair, radiant complexion, and entire get-up provoked the admiration of all who saw her. Nor did they dream that the lady ever presented herself in any other guise, or that she had recourse to art in order to enhance and transform her naturally charming appearance. Contrary to his usual custom, Gregory Staines was also present at breakfast, and Miss Stratton's eyes gleamed so triumphantly when she observed his amazed admiration of herself that she deemed it advisable to veil their brightness by looking down at Briny, who, as was his usual custom when permitted to do so, was sitting beside his mistress in his dual capacity of guardian and beloved protégé. She had had considerable fear lest Gregory Staines should see something about her appearance that would lead him to couple her with either Miss Annie Cory or the pseudo governess. But as she caught his badly-veiled glances of approval her heart glowed with satisfaction.

"If one of my plans fails," she thought, "the other must succeed. I came here with the deliberate intention of personating a modified Delilah, and I seem to have hit upon the type of feminine attractiveness most pleasing in his eyes. I feel sure now that I can fascinate him. But I am not quite so sure that I can veil my natural repulsion to him successfully. It will be just dreadful to feign the captive syren with a man who possesses my deadly hatred. But I would do even more than that for Harley."

As she concluded this reflection Miss Stratton raised her eyes, as if furtively, to Mr. Staines's face, and then glanced down again, apparently in sudden confusion. Her embarrassment was so well feigned that Mr. Staines experienced a sudden thrill of satisfaction and flattered vanity.

"Why, I do believe she is struck with me," he thought, complacently. "She is a rattling beauty, too, by Jove! I wonder if she has got any money? If appearances go for anything, she has. She might prove quite a good catch. But I must be careful, or the little Dollman may get rusty, and I don't want to cook my goose in that quarter yet."

Mr. and Mrs. Everton had written to say that they would not come back for another week. Mr. Grice had had an early breakfast, and was already off to the office in which he spent most of his days. Mrs. Dollman had some housekeeping duties to attend to after breakfast was over, and there was, therefore, a capital opportunity for a tête-à-tête. Of this opportunity, nothing loth, Mr. Staines availed himself. Miss Stratton had seated herself on a chair at a small table standing at the window. This window, as we already know, overlooked the garden at the back of the house, and as the young lady, leaning her arms upon the table, asked his opinion concerning the identity of first one flower and then another, to all of which she professed herself a stranger, it seemed the most natural thing in the world for Gregory Staines to take the chair facing Miss Stratton, on the other side of the table, in order to converse with her more naturally and pleasantly.

"Do you love flowers?" he asked, greedily gazing at the exquisite contour of the face within so short a distance of him.

"I love everything nice," was the reply.

"You make me feel envious," he said.

"Envious? Why, how can that be?" inquired Una, with a wonderful assumption of ingenuousness.

"Say rather, how can it be otherwise. Perhaps you do not know what it feels like to be loved by such a being as yourself. Your very presence is intoxicating."

"Mr. Staines! Do you forget that we have not known each other an hour, and you are already paying me compliments?"

"An hour! Is it only an hour since? I suppose it is. And yet I feel as if I had known you all my life. It seems almost unaccountable, doesn't it? There must be some natural affinity between you and me."

And Miss Stratton permitted the man to talk on in this strain of offensive familiarity! Nay more, she encouraged it, for not only did she smile, apparently well pleased, at his vapid compliments, but she allowed herself to cast upon him such a languishing glance as fully excused his belief that he was exceedingly well pleasing in her sight.

"By Jove! she must be awfully struck!" he thought, gleefully. "I do believe she is actually making love to me. I am not particularly inclined to matrimony, but a subrosa liaison with a beauty like this would vary my life very pleasantly. I mean to go in for a little fun, and if this young lady is fool enough to throw herself into my arms, why—it's her look out, not mine. I can easily clear, whenever I want to back out of it."

ELIZABETH BURGOYNE CORBETT

After this Mr. Staines would fain have continued talking to Una. But she, apparently of an impulsive nature, suddenly announced that she had work to do in her own room, and would not remain with him any longer. He, emboldened by her complaisant behaviour, eagerly sought to detain her awhile longer, and even grasped her right hand between both his own, as he pleaded for a little more time with her. As soon as she felt him touch her, Una turned her face from him, shuddering violently in an agony of repulsion, and Briny sprang to his feet, growling in a threatening manner.

"Be quiet, Briny," said Una; "don't you know a friend when you see one?"

Of course, Mr. Staines took the reproof administered to Briny as a direct compliment to himself. He also mistook Una's shudder for a thrill of delight invoked by the contact between his hand and hers, and congratulated himself triumphantly upon the easy conquest he had made. Indeed, so sure of his ground did he feel that he resisted the girl's attempt to withdraw her hand, squeezed it tenderly, and whispered confidentially, "We can have a chat this afternoon, cannot we, Miss Stratton?"

Miss Stratton's reply was such a languishing and apparently love-stricken look that, but for the threatening attitude of Briny, who evidently did not like him, he would there and then have attempted to kiss her.

"Will you come out for a walk this afternoon?" he asked. "It will not do to let these people see too much, I suppose. I can meet you at the end of the street, and will show you the sights of the neighbourhood. Say, will you come?"

"At what time?"

"Will three o'clock suit you?"

"There, I hear the landlady coming. She mustn't see you squeezing my hand."

"By Jove, no. She might be jealous, eh! At three o'clock, then?"

"Come, Briny, I want you to go out with me. We have some work to do this morning, and I have an appointment for three o'clock this afternoon."

This was all the answer vouchsafed to Mr. Staines, beyond another bewildering glance as Miss Stratton hurriedly quitted the room, followed by the faithful Briny. But he understood its meaning perfectly, and knew that he might rely upon getting the pleasant walk he had proposed.

"Rather quick work," he mused, stroking his well-waxed moustache, and indulging in a smirk of gratified vanity. "I've never gone in for lady-killing much. But it seems to me that I can have things pretty much my own way with women, if I like to lay myself out to please them. First the pretty young widow, and then the beautiful artist. And I had half a notion of marrying the widow! What a fool I should have been today if I had been already booked! Good Lord! this girl isn't fit to leave home by herself. She'll be like wax in my hands, and I can clear out when I get tired of her, unless she proves to have plenty of money, in which case I shall make it my business to get hold of it, sooner or later."

Meanwhile, the subject of his complaisant musings was in her own room, with the door locked, and was walking backwards and forwards in an agony of passion such as would have surprised him, if he could have seen it. She rubbed her right hand violently with her pocket handkerchief, and gave vent to short inarticulate cries of fury.

"I thought I could bear it," she panted, hoarsely, "I believed I could endure anything for Harley's sake, and to bring this perjured thief and murderer to justice. I have overrated my strength, for the contamination of his touch has nearly driven me mad. And yet I acted so well that I really believe that he imagines me to have fallen hopelessly in love with him! I am sure he also thinks me infatuated and pliant enough to be a willing tool in his hands. Upon my word, it doesn't take much manœuvring to throw dust in the eyes of a vain man."

Miss Stratton muttered a good deal more to the same purpose, and then, having calmed down a little, began to wash her hands, for she was not satisfied with merely rubbing off Mr. Staines' touch. Then, having made sure that her toilet and disguise were all perfect, she ascertained from Mrs. Dollman the time at which she would be expected in to lunch, and, carrying a portfolio with her, went out, ostensibly to sketch. Her real purpose, however, was to hunt about until she found a shop in which she could buy or order a few local sketches, as nearly in the same style as some English sketches that she had brought with her as possible. She was fortunate enough to secure just what she wanted, and at a price, too, which made her wonder how the artist could possibly make a living at that sort of work.

Returning to the house, she found that it was near lunch time, and that Mr. Staines, contrary to his usual custom, intended to grace the board with his presence. But he was very cautious in his behaviour, and Mrs. Dollman's sharp eyes could not detect more admiration on his part for the beautiful stranger than was consistent with the fact that she was a previously unknown new arrival. On her side Miss Stratton was a pattern of discreetness, and bestowed nearly all her attention upon the pretty little mistress of the house.

After lunch was over Mrs. Dollman begged to see Miss Stratton's sketches. The portfolio, therefore, was fetched out, and the little drawings it contained were duly admired. The local views were not shown yet. They were intended to account for time that Miss Stratton expected to devote to other pursuits than sketching, and would not be shown at all if events developed themselves as quickly as she hoped. Truth to tell, she was not very clever with pencil or brush, and such artistic achievements as she was able to show were due to the "amour propre" of her drawing master. He, knowing that in nineteen cases out of twenty it is usual for young ladies to discard their school pursuits as soon as their education is pronounced complete, thought it a pity that they should not have something to show their fond parents for all the money spent upon them, and made a point of doing their work himself if he found that his pupils showed no special aptitude for it. In this way he built himself a fine reputation as an art teacher, for the vanity of the majority of his pupils forbade them to betray the fact that they had really had very little to do with the production of the pictures bearing their signature. Miss Stratton had not started upon her present enterprise without having first matured her plans, and she had even taken the precaution to change the initials of the little pictures with which she meant to support her assumption of the role of an artist. But, all used as she was becoming to the necessity for a certain amount of deception, she felt very uncomfortable when listening to the praises lavished upon work to which she could lay very little claim.

When this little farce was over there was a general adjournment, and Miss Stratton betook herself to her own room to prepare for the intended excursion, in the rôle of a complaisant inamorata, with her mortal enemy. The latter, after meeting her outside, as per arrangement, did all in his power to amuse his companion, and was highly pleased with his afternoon's entertainment. When he was once more left alone, at the end of the street leading to Mrs. Dollman's house, he was vainer than he had ever been in his life before, and anticipated not the slightest drawback to the success of the love affair upon which he had just entered.

But Miss Stratton's feelings ran in a different groove. While apparently quite happy in the company of Mr. Staines, she was careful not to agree to any scheme of enjoyment that involved retirement from the public thoroughfares. While there she felt herself safe, and did not hesitate to befool Mr. Staines so egregiously that he already regarded her as his willing prey. She was, however, by no means quite satisfied with her day's work so far. During the course of her conversation she had casually mentioned her desire to inspect Gibraltar under pleasant guardianship. But the gentleman showed such a decided aversion to the idea of visiting that place that the prospect of luring him there seemed as yet but a remote one.

Now, as her sole object in thus cultivating his society was to find an opportunity of persuading him to visit the fortress, in order that she might have his arrest effected upon English ground, it is not surprising that the prospect of failure in this direction should cause her some disquietude. A prolonged flirtation with the scoundrel would be unendurable. Still, she was determined to give the game a fair trial, and if it failed, she could but hope that as "Mr. Bootle" she would be more successful. Briny had been taken out with her, but could not be persuaded to show any liking for Mr. Staines.

"I am sorry to be unable to give you my company this evening, but hope to spend several hours with you tomorrow. Had I known of your arrival, I would not have made the appointment to which I am bound to attend tonight. But we mean to have a jolly big day together tomorrow, eh?"

Mr. Staines went his way, very well satisfied with the answer he got, though Miss Stratton's comment upon his curious way of preferring his request might not have pleased him.

"He is sorry to be unable to give me a share of his company this evening! Rather cool, forsooth, even for a vain fool like that. I doubt I have acted only too well. I should have coquetted and played with him, and made him think that, to please me, it would be necessary to accede to all my requests. Yet no! The man is too coarse to be captivated by modesty, and I do not despair by any means. Poor Harley! It is well for his peace of mind that he does not know how far I have to stoop to help him."

XIX

Sergeant-Major Twiley Has a Surprise

S o you are not playing tonight?"

"No; I have been thinking over something you said to me last night, and fancy that a confidential conversation might prove profitable to both of us. Suppose we slip out and compare notes?"

"I don't mind. We can easily come back if we wish to do so."

The speakers were Gregory Staines and Mr. Bootle, the latter being the first to open the conversation. As they walked briskly onwards, he gradually betrayed his real character to his companion, or, rather, he would have done so had Mr. Bootle not thoroughly gauged it beforehand.

"How long have you lived in this part of the world, Mr. Bootle?"

"Only a few weeks. I am not in the habit of staying too long in places likely to prove unprofitable. I'm a bird of passage, fond of migrating, in season or out of season."

"And in what way do you expect to make this place profitable?"

"H'm! That's a bit of a secret yet. I don't believe in being indiscreet."

"In other words, you distrust me?"

"You put your question in a somewhat abrupt style. Still, as you are no doubt aware, there are some ways of earning a living of which the authorities have a nasty knack of disapproving. You strike me as just the sort of man whom I want to get hold of. Yet I have no guarantee that such is really the case, and I have too much at stake to risk failure by being unduly confidential."

"Look here, Mr. Bootle. Say right out what you want to say. I don't think you have any real doubts as to my likelihood of proving just the sort of man you want. If there is money in the job, and I am to have my share in it, I'm in with you, provided there isn't too much risk to be run; but you need not imagine that I'll be a mere tool for anybody. Acting partner on equal terms, if you like, and I am your man. Now, what do you want me to do?"

"Not much. You are lucky at cards. I would like to share your luck."

"I see. You have something in immediate view. Who is the pigeon to be plucked?"

"A young fellow who is visiting at Gibraltar just now. He lately succeeded to a fortune that he did not expect, and is now doing his level best to make ducks and drakes of it. He is outrageously fond of cards, and loses with the best grace imaginable. It hurts me to see the way in which he is enriching all sorts of cads, and I have often wondered how I could divert a share of this stream of wealth in my direction. Last night I arrived at a possible solution of my perplexities. I saw you play. Without hinting that your methods of playing are not all square and above board, I must say that I could not help noticing the wonderful facility with which you were always able to produce winning cards. Do you think you can be as successful with anyone?"

"If it is worth my while."

"Then will you honestly turn over half your winnings to me, if I introduce this stranger to you?"

"With all my heart! All I stipulate is that you lose no time over it. How are you going to manage it?"

"Well, the matter does not strike me as very difficult. I have had a few games with your pigeon. But I am such a duffer at play that I need never hope to make my fortune in that line. Suppose I try to persuade him to come to Lina? You could be on the look out; I would introduce you; and your own cleverness could do the rest."

"When shall it be? Tomorrow night?"

"That I cannot say. If I were Mr. Danvers' bosom friend it might be straightforward sailing. As it is, I am only a new acquaintance, although I have done my best to ingratiate myself with him. If I invite him over here it must be with some special excuse. A little supper party would do it. You could invite the gentleman who seemed so partial to you last night to make a fourth, and I'll stand exes."

Mr. Staines seized this plan with avidity, and almost overwhelmed his informant with questions, all of which related in some way or other to the supposed habits and circumstances of the myth which had been invoked solely in Harley Riddell's interests. Satisfied eventually that a very good haul was probably in store for him, he went on his way rejoicing. Mr. Bootle would not return with him to the hotel, but pleaded that his only sensible course was to return to Gibraltar, whence he professed to have come, in order to endeavour to make an appointment with Mr. Danvers.

But the reader hardly needs to be told that Gibraltar saw nothing of Mr. Bootle that evening. On the contrary, he went straight to the lodgings that he found so comfortable and convenient. Briny was waiting for him with his usual watchfulness, and was very glad to find that he was not doomed to spend the whole evening alone. Instead of going to bed

Mr. Bootle carefully changed his apparel, and emerged presently from the room attired as Miss Una Stratton.

"You are in nice time for supper, Miss Stratton," said Mrs. Dollman. "I hope your headache has left you."

"Thank you," was the reply. "I feel much better now. Do you mind my bringing Briny into the room with me? He has had to be very quiet since tea-time."

"Certainly not. He's a jolly dog, whom to know is to like. Eh, Briny? Miss Stratton, let me introduce my brother-in-law to you. This is Mr. Twiley."

"Yes, I have already heard of you, Mr. Twiley, and am pleased to make your acquaintance."

So said the young lady upon whom the sergeant-major's eyes were fixed with unaffected admiration. And when she said she was pleased to see him she meant it, too. For she had already been revolving a plot in her mind in which the sergeant-major played a prominent part, and her first glance at him convinced her that he was a man whom she could trust. He was in the very position to afford her certain aid which she desired, and it was a great relief to her to find that he was just the sort of man she had imagined Mrs. Twiley's husband to be. So she resolved to lose no time in taking him into her confidence, as she needed an able coadjutor at once. But even urgent confidences must be repressed until a seasonable opportunity for their disclosure occurs, and Miss Stratton began to fear that her designs were fated to be baulked for the time being.

At last, however, she saw a fair chance of speaking, for, supper being over, the dining-room was left to the occupation of Miss Stratton, Mrs. Dollman, and Sergeant-Major Twiley. The latter had come over unexpectedly, having had some commission in the town to execute, and still had a little time to spare ere he need return to quarters.

"Have you time to sit down here a little while, Mrs. Dollman?" asked Miss Stratton, not without a slight touch of nervousness in her voice. "I have something very important to tell you, and I am anxious that your brother-in-law should listen to me also. But the door must be carefully closed, lest we be overheard. You will appreciate my anxiety on this score when I tell you that life itself may depend upon our caution. Nay, do not look so dubious. I have much to confess to you, but my confessions are not discreditable to myself. At least, I do not believe it likely that you will think so when I have told you my story. I am here, not in the character of a fugitive, but of a pursuer."

"And whom are you pursuing?" asked the sergeant-major, his curiosity considerably aroused.

"You know the man very well. He lives in this house."

"Impossible!"

"Not a bit of it. I have known the man as Hugh Stavanger, as Paul Torrens, and as Harry Morton, and have at last, I hope, run him to earth as Gregory Staines."

"Why, Miss Stratton," said Mrs. Dollman, with some excitement, although she obeyed the warning finger held up, and modulated her voice to a low pitch, "you and he were the best of friends yesterday, and today, also, anyone seeing you together would have thought you were old friends."

"Poor girl! I imagined I had been too careful to have betrayed any apparent familiarity with Staines," thought Miss Stratton; "but 'to the jealous, trifles light as air are proofs as strong as Holy Writ.' It is well I came here before this poor child's heart was wounded too sorely. She is a brave girl, I am sure, and her farcical admiration for this scoundrel will turn to disgust as soon as she learns his real character."

It will be noticed that our heroine spoke of the young widow as if she herself were the senior of the two. But wisdom and self-reliance are not always dependant upon age, and the younger girl's experience and courage had given her sounder judgment than is possessed by the average woman of forty. Aloud she said:—

"Yes, I flatter myself that I have acted my part well this time. He hates me, fears me, and flees from me as if I were grim death. And yet he is ready to fall in love with me."

"I don't understand," said Phœbe Dollman, with a troubled look in her eyes. "How can he both hate you and love you?"

"That is easily explained. My real name is Annie Cory, and my sole objects in life at present are to bring this scoundrel to book for a series of crimes which he has committed, and to liberate an innocent man from penal servitude. Hugh Stavanger—or shall we call him Gregory Staines for the nonce?—would know me very well if my disguise were not so perfect. But my natural appearance falls very short of what you see now, as I will soon show you, if you will cover that window more securely. I was watching you through it last night, and he might follow my example tonight."

Annie's hearers were too astonished and mystified to say much. But they did as she asked them, and attentively watched the transformation wrought in her appearance. By-and-bye they saw the girl as we first knew her—dark-haired, and of brunette complexion.

"You see what a wig can do," she smiled, "and a little knowledge in the art of making up. Even my figure, gait, and voice have been altered in the service of justice. But you would be most astonished if you saw me conversing in a familiar manner with Mr. Staines in still another character—that of a moderately tall, slim young man, with a lovely dark moustache. Patent cork elevators are a fine aid to height. But I see you are dreadfully mystified, so will tell you everything, feeling sure that I can depend upon you to help me. One word more. I am not an artist, nor ever will be. But I have plenty of money at command, and any plan that you may suggest will not fail through lack of finances."

For fully half an hour not a sound was heard in the room, except Annie rapidly relating her history, and describing the true character of Gregory Staines, and for fully ten minutes longer the sergeant-major sat with compressed lips and fiercely-knitted brows, intent upon inventing a scheme to circumvent the villain.

"I have it," he exclaimed, at last, bringing his fist fiercely down upon the table. "You will never succeed in decoying him into Gibraltar. But we won't waste time over him. If he won't go willingly into the arms of the English authorities, he must be made to go."

"And how can that be managed?"

"Easily. He will be rather a big child to deal with, but I guess he is nearly at the end of his tether—we will kidnap him."

XX

A Critical Game

The day after the one in which so many confidences had been bestowed upon Mrs. Dollman and her friends by Miss Stratton was one of considerable anxiety to the latter. Poor little Phœbe, although one of the brightest and nicest women in the world, was a very bad actress, and she could not for the life of her treat Mr. Staines with the same cordiality as before, although warned of the immense importance of self-restraint. Personally, she did not feel as aggrieved as might have been expected, for her heart had never been touched, although she had been led to admire a man who knew very well how to be fascinating when he pleased. Now she felt extremely disgusted with herself for having been pleased with the flattery her lodger had bestowed upon her, and the young fellow of whom her brother-in-law had spoken as an honest admirer now stood a good chance of getting his innings.

But, try as she might, she could not help showing something of the detestation which a knowledge of Gregory Staines' real character had awakened in her. As he sat at her breakfast-table, she pictured poor Harley Riddell languishing for his crime in prison. And when, after being out for a few hours, he faced her at the dinner-table, she conjured Hilton's spectre behind him, and was seized with such a trembling that she let the soup-ladle fall back into the soup-tureen with a crash that cracked the latter, and a splash that covered the tablecloth and her dress with the hot liquid. Suspecting the real cause of her emotion, Miss Stratton, who was sitting near her, pressed her foot warningly upon hers, and exclaimed solicitously—

"You seem quite shaky today, Mrs. Dollman. Are you not well?"

"Oh, yes, I am quite well, thank you," replied the little widow. "But I'm all in a tremble with something or other. It's the heat, I think."

The heat! And it had been found necessary to have a good fire in the dining-room, as everybody was complaining of the cold. Miss Stratton felt the moment to be a critical one. But she did not lose her self-possession, although she saw the sudden suspicion which leaped into the eyes of Gregory Staines, who, with knife and fork slightly raised from his plate, was sitting immovable, mutely questioning the faces of the blundering Phœbe and herself.

"Really," she laughed, "if you go on like this, I shall swear that you are in love, and that your inamorato has had the bad taste to transfer his affections elsewhere. Fancy complaining of the cold one minute, and being all of a tremble with the heat the next! Those are genuine love symptoms—I've felt them myself."

As Miss Stratton spoke, with such apparent disregard of Phœbe's feelings, she darted an admiring and meaning look at Gregory Staines, which at once put that gentleman at his ease again for a little while.

"The little fool has seen that the artist is more in my line, and is jealous," he mused. "But what of that? She can't harm me, though she may make things deucedly uncomfortable for me here. Query, will it really pay me to break with her? That remains to be seen. I'm by no means sure that Miss Stratton has money that I can secure, or that it would be as good a prospect to take up with her as to settle down here, with Phœbe to keep me. I think I must retain both irons in the fire for a few days longer. Stratton is so awfully infatuated that she will be only too glad to condone a flirtation with Phœbe."

In pursuance of this train of thought, Mr. Staines became very solicitous about Mrs. Dollman's state of health, smiled quite tenderly at her, suggested that she should lie down to compose her nerves, and offered to take all the labours of carving off her hands. But it was not in Phœbe's nature to restrain her feelings, and when he accidentally touched her hand in taking the carving-knife from her, she sprang away from him with such an agony of horror and repulsion in her face, that he could no longer doubt her real sentiments towards him, and everyone at the table could see that there was more beneath the surface than met the eye. As for Gregory Staines, he was thunderstruck, although he was able to keep both his actions and his facial expression under admirable control.

"She has been told something about me," was his savage inward comment. "Somebody has betrayed me, and the little idiot has been made the sharer of a secret that she cannot keep. Betrayal means enmity, and the presence of a betrayal argues the near proximity of an enemy. I have but one enemy whom I need fear, and she has been cleverly put off the scent. And, yet, who knows? The devil himself must be in her, for she has followed and traced me to all sorts of places, and why not here? Good God! I never thought of it! Surely it can't be this woman who has flung herself at my head as if I were the God of Love in the flesh? But, after all, even if it were, what can she do to me? She dare not move openly, for no plans for my arrest can be made effectual on Spanish territory. If she has really traced me, I am safe for today, at all events. I must meet her with her own weapons, and if I find that Miss Stratton and my arch-enemy are one and the same, may the Lord have mercy on her soul!"

The object of his meditations was not slow to observe that Mr. Staines had suddenly received food for thought, and was not deceived, even though he kept his countenance so cleverly.

"I must be careful not to place myself for any length of time in his power," she thought. "He is quite capable of murdering me, if his suspicions of my true identity are assured, and with me all hope of Harley's salvation would die."

And yet all this bye-play was unnoticed by the other boarders sitting at the table. Mrs. Dollman was a little nervous, and Mr. Staines was good-naturedly solicitous on her behalf. That was all. An hour later the room was empty of all but Miss Stratton and Mr. Staines, and the two were outwardly as enamoured of each other as yesterday. She wished to amuse him, lull his suspicions, and engage his attention until it was time to meet her in the evening, in her assumed character of Mr. Bootle. He was bent upon watching every gesture and movement of hers, and upon comparing her personality with that of the girl he suspected her to be.

Thus the afternoon wore away, and tea-time arrived. Miss Stratton had declined an invitation to have a walk with Mr. Staines, saying that she preferred a tête-à-tête by the fireside, and she had found an opportunity to warn Mrs. Dollman against saying or doing anything that could ruin the plans which were being matured with a view to capturing Mr. Staines. He was apparently as complaisant and love-stricken as ever, and both played at exchanging confidences which bore very little relation to their actual experiences. When, shortly before tea-time, Miss Stratton adjourned to her own room, she imagined that her influence over the man whom she was befooling was almost as strong as it was yesterday.

But he was deeper than she gave him credit for being, and had made an important discovery. While toying with her hair, and enthusiastically admiring its golden brilliance, he had satisfied himself that it was an artificial covering which hid the darker glory which was her natural heritage. For one brief period our heroine's life was in immediate danger, and the reason it was spared then was because her enemy had promptly resolved to seek an opportunity likely to be fraught with less danger to himself.

They saw each other at the tea-table awhile later, and Miss Stratton was looking lovelier than ever—so lovely that, though he hated her, Gregory Staines felt himself moved by the wildest admiration of her outward charms, for her eyes sparkled and her cheeks glowed with the excitement of her conviction that at last the hour of her triumph was near at hand. Mrs. Twiley was here again. She had brought a message from her husband, and fully understood the importance of the step he contemplated taking that night. The adventure he proposed was a somewhat risky one. But she had every confidence in his courage and discretion, and was, moreover, much more capable of keeping a secret than her sister. Gregory Staines watched her narrowly, but could not detect any embarrassment in her intercourse with him, or any covert collusion between her and Miss Stratton.

"She knows nothing about me," he thought, "and she does not seem to get on very well with the girl who is masquerading here as an artist. But that sort of thing is only natural with women. They are always jealous of anyone prettier than themselves. By heaven, I wish I had really the chance I fancied I had of winning this superb creature. Fancy having a gambling-house, with a wife like that at the head of affairs! Why, there would be no end of a fortune to be made. But it is useless to think of it, if she is really Annie Cory. If! Why, there is a doubt yet, in spite of appearances. I can't see what her motive in making love to me can be, after all. What could she gain by it, so long as I stayed in Spain? It strikes me that I had better not be too rash. I will watch and wait. If my suspicions are unfounded, so much the better. If not, so much the worse—for her!"

Meanwhile, Miss Stratton excused herself to Mrs. Dollman, and announced her intention of spending the evening in her room, as she had a great many letters to write. Arrived there, she found plenty to occupy her for half an hour. At the end of that time Mrs. Twiley came to her by prearrangement, and was utterly astonished to watch the metamorphosis effected in her appearance while she was there.

"Why, you make me feel inclined to run away again," she laughed. "It's dreadfully compromising to be here alone with you. Suppose a servant, or one of the other boarders saw me, the consequences would be awful! My reputation would be gone, and poor, dear Twiley's only consolation would be a divorce. But, seriously, it is wonderful to think of all you have done and are doing for the sake of your lover. I hope you will be successful in all your plans, and some day I expect the pleasure of seeing Mr. Riddell enjoying liberty and happiness once more."

"Thank you so much," said the lady addressed, who was, to all appearances, a man again, to wit, Mr. Bootle, "Whenever that happy day arrives, believe me, I shall esteem it a sacred duty to bring him to see all who have helped us in our dark days."

"In fact, you will come here for your honeymoon."

"Honeymoon! I dare not think of such happiness while he is languishing in prison. See, would you like to judge how he looked only a year ago?"

As she spoke, the girl handed a photograph of a handsome, smiling young fellow to her visitor, at which the latter gazed with a mist gathering in her eyes.

"And this," she was next told, "is the brother who has been foully murdered."

It struck Mrs. Twiley that the brother was even a nobler type of manhood than the unfortunate lover, but she had too much tact to betray that opinion, though she looked long and earnestly at the lineaments of one who was supposed to have come to so sad an end.

Then the whole of the evening's intended work was gone over again in detail, not an item being overlooked that could conduce to either success or failure. Everything being at length arranged, Mrs. Twiley rejoined her sister, and "Mr. Bootle" prepared to sally forth on her evening's adventures, of which she by no means underestimated the possible peril. But the courage engendered by devotion to others transcends all other courage in its nobility and strength, and not the faintest twinge of fear assailed our heroine, as, feeling added security in her capital disguise, she told Briny to remain on guard, and stepped out of the window into the garden, whence she presently emerged into the lane, and thence into the open street.

But what was that dark object creeping in her footsteps, and dodging nearer and nearer to her? It was no friend, that is certain, as he would not have slunk out of sight so promptly everytime that there was any likelihood of his being observed. Had "Mr. Bootle" looked round, he, or she, if the reader prefers, might possibly have seen a mortal enemy, armed with a knife, and carefully watching his opportunity for removing the one whom he feared.

And had Mr. Staines looked round, he would have noticed a pursuer in his turn, one who disliked him already, and who would not hesitate to protect "Mr. Bootle" at the cost of his life. This was the faithful Briny, who, for once, had disobeyed his owner by following her when forbidden to do so. His consciousness of wrong-doing made him linger in the background. But he was none the less a valuable protector, even though his presence was unsuspected.

Yet neither of the beings whom he was following looked round, and neither one nor the other dreamed of danger behind, so anxious were they to reach the goal that lay before them.

XXI

"Ware Assassin!"

There was a somewhat obscure and badly-lighted stretch of road to traverse ere Mr. Bootle could reach his destination, which was the hotel so much frequented by Gregory Staines. Very often, especially at certain times of the day, the place was tolerably well frequented. But it chanced sometimes that it was comparatively deserted, and upon this fact Gregory Staines counted for his opportunity to get rid of his enemy. That that enemy was a woman was not a deterrent circumstance with him. She was more dangerous to him than ten ordinary men, by virtue of her extraordinary perseverance, her devotion to her lover, her unflinching courage, and the keenness with which she pursued her self-imposed mission. Therefore, she must be rendered harmless, and there was but one way of effecting this desirable result.

"It's her own fault," he muttered. "If she will throw herself into the lion's jaws, she has none but herself to blame if he closes his teeth upon her. By Jove, what a schemer she is! She hesitates at nothing. Fancy making love to me, in order to bewitch me into acceding to any request she might make of me. I know now why she hinted her desire to see Gibraltar in my company. She wanted to inveigle me into English territory; but that game's off, my dear. And then how extraordinarily well she is got up now! I should never have suspected 'Mr. Bootle's' *bona fides* if that little fool of a Dollman had not roused my suspicions about 'Miss Stratton.' Being suspicious, it was natural that I should watch her, and that I should listen at her window. But I shall never forget my amazement at discovering how completely I had been hoodwinked. Yet I am sure that my previous failure to penetrate her dual disguise must be attributed to her superior cleverness, not to my denseness. This makes it all the more imperative to remove her—and now I see my chance."

The next moment he had stealthily sprung forward, and with arm upraised, was about to plunge a knife into Mr. Bootle's back, when there was a sudden rush, and he felt himself borne to the ground by a heavy mass which threw itself against him. With a startled cry he flung out his arms, and made a frantic effort to save himself from falling, the knife which he meant to have used to such deadly purpose dropping from his nerveless grasp. But his struggle was useless, and he lay gasping with terror, while Briny (for he it was who had thus opportunely come to the rescue) held him down, and growled murderous things. Mr. Bootle had turned round as soon as he heard the commotion behind him, and, recognising Briny, guessed at once what was the matter.

"The dastard has intended to kill me, or to stun me, thinking me a fit subject for robbery," was his first thought. But presently, on approaching nearer, he recognised his foe, and realised that his disguise was penetrated. Like lightning, however, the idea flashed through his brain that even yet it would be good policy to appear to be unaware of Gregory Staines' discovery, and to pretend to be ignorant of the motive of Briny's attack upon him.

"Briny! Briny!" he called hurriedly. "Mind what you are doing. Off! I say. Off at once! This is a friend!"

Briny, in obedience to the voice which he knew and loved through every attempt at disguising it, drew himself off the recumbent figure of the man, who was dreading lest he should use his fangs, and whom terror was rendering passive under his weight. But that he relinquished his prey with great reluctance was quite evident, and he growled menacingly as Gregory Staines rose to his feet, with a sickly attempt to endorse his foe's assumption of the unreasonableness of Briny's attack upon him.

"That is a nasty brute to fall foul of," he said angrily. "There is no telling what mischief he might have done me, if you had not been handy. I noticed who was in front of me, and hurried forward to overtake you, when I was hurled to the ground without any ceremony. But how do you happen to be acquainted with this dog? And how is it that he seems to know you so well?"

"My dear sir, I can easily explain away your mystification on that score. Briny belongs to a very dear friend of mine, a Miss Stratton, whose arrival in Lina I have been expecting for a week. The presence of Briny shows that my friend is here now, and I shall probably see her tomorrow."

Such was Mr. Bootle's remark, given in a calm and composed voice, which certainly surprised Staines by the astonishing nerve it evinced. That the composure of the voice was somewhat belied by an irrepressible trembling of the limbs for a few moments was not apparent to the latter, and he felt all the more savage at his failure to secure the extermination of so implacable an enemy.

"I wonder what the game is now," he thought. "It can't be that I'm expected to swallow this pretence of being friendly. There is still some further plotting going on, and it is deemed necessary to keep me befooled a little while longer. I think I will play the unsuspecting chicken. But I'm too clever to be caught."

Anyone noticing the further progress of this antagonistic couple towards the hotel would hardly have imagined them to be either great friends or great enemies. For they walked, conversing together, fully a yard apart, and each kept a wary eye upon the other, the dog carefully watching Mr. Staines' every movement. Arrived at the hotel, the pair appeared to be on the same terms as they had been yesterday, and soon began to discuss the business which ostensibly brought them both here.

"How about your gambling friend at Gibraltar, Mr. Bootle?" was the query addressed to him.

"Just as rackety as ever," he replied. "The money being squandered like water, and any amount of hawks hovering round in search of prey."

"Ourselves included, eh?"

"Yes, ourselves included."

"And how is the prey to be got at?"

"By following out the plan suggested yesterday evening. I have seen Mr. Danvers today, and he has accepted my invitation to supper. I had some difficulty in inducing him to agree to come here. He wanted me to hold the affair at my rooms in Gibraltar, but I told him that I had invited a fellow who did not care to show himself on English territory, and with whose company he would be delighted."

"And how do you know that I would not care to go to Gibraltar?"

"Natural inference, my dear sir. Perhaps I shouldn't be too fond of the place myself if my real name was known there."

"So you masquerade under an alias?"

"Certainly. Just as you do."

"Precisely. But I would like to set your mind at rest on one point. I have not the slightest objection to go to Gibraltar. So if Mr. Danvers objects to coming here I will meet him on his own ground. Did you hold out any other inducement to Mr. Danvers to tempt his presence at our proposed supper?"

"Yes; I told him that my friend Miss Stratton would be present, and promised him a great treat, for she is both clever and handsome."

"Exceedingly so, Mr. Bootle. Cleverer than most people would be inclined to believe; but even such abnormal cleverness as hers over-reaches itself sometimes."

"Possibly. She isn't infallible. But after next Friday her mission in Spain will be ended, and she can then return to safer quarters."

For sometime after this remark very little was said. Then Mr. Staines, seeing an acquaintance of his at the other end of the saloon, asked Mr. Bootle to excuse him for five minutes, and left him to meditate the progress of affairs by himself.

"I wonder how much and how little he knows," the latter mused. "And I also wonder whether he really swallows my yarn about the supper. He has discovered who I really am. Of that I am convinced. But does he also know that Mr. Bootle and Miss Stratton are one and the same individual, and that it is a serious strain on my vocal organs to talk so much in an assumed voice? His professed willingness to go to Gibraltar does not deceive me. He knows that the whole story about Mr. Danvers is pure fiction. Knowing this, he is also convinced that I have an ulterior motive behind my apparent friendliness. I have hinted that Miss Stratton has no further business here after Friday. He imagines me to have some plot on foot, which will take until Friday to mature, although this is only Monday. If I am not mistaken, he is now plotting with that villainous-looking fellow who is with him to get rid of me before that time, and, were I remaining here, I might expect another attack upon my life. But after tonight, my friend, you will be harmless."

Meanwhile Mr. Staines was rapidly explaining as much of the situation as suited him to the individual before-mentioned.

"Don't look round," he said. "You saw me come in with the young fellow I have just left. Do you think that he would prove difficult to tackle from behind?"

"Not if to tackle him were worth one's while, mister. Is he in your way?"

"Very much so."

"What would his removal be worth to you?"

"Twenty pounds. Ten now, and ten on completion of the job."

"I think you may depend upon me to conduct the business satisfactorily. But twenty quid is too little. Double it and put half down, and I'm your man."

"Indeed I won't. The affair wouldn't be worth all that to me. The youngster is in my way, but his removal is not necessary. Twenty pounds it is, or nothing."

"Very well, then. Nothing it shall be. I want to cut this and go to America, but I may as well be hard up here a bit longer as reach America without a penny, and if you won't give forty, I won't take the risk."

Gregory Staines hated to part with so much money, for every penny it cost him to preserve his liberty made him think that his crime had not brought him a life whose pleasures were equivalent to the penalties exacted from him. But he reflected that he would never be safe while so determined an enemy lived, and resolved upon what he deemed a last sacrifice.

"Very well," he said at last, "you shall have what you ask. But mind you don't hit the wrong man, and watch the dog. Your best plan will be to wait until you see us go out together, and then watch your chance. If necessary, I will help you, for it's about time this game was ended."

A few more arrangements were made, the hired assassin received half his fee, and Mr. Staines returned to his intended victim, remarking: "What a nuisance duns are! I owed that fellow a few shillings, and he had the impudence to insist upon being paid tonight."

"That's the worst of dealing with common people," said Mr. Bootle, carelessly. "But we have talked over all preliminaries about our supper party, and about the pigeon whom we intend to pluck. On Wednesday night you must be in good trim, as Danvers is sure to bring a lot of money with him."

"And where are you off to now?"

"To my lodgings."

"Do you mean to take the dog with you?"

"No, I think he had better be sent home. He will be able to find Miss Stratton, and tomorrow I shall hear from her. She knows where to write to."

"I have a better plan than that. Miss Stratton has come to stay at the house I am in. Come with me, and see her this evening. It is not yet late."

This plan was readily agreed to, and the two set out together, each knowing the other to be plotting his safety, and each warily watching his companion's every movement, the dog being quite as watchful as his companions.

There was also another form carefully gauging his chances of making the attack by which he hoped to put another twenty pounds in his pocket. This individual was so exceedingly anxious not to miss his opportunity, that he failed to notice sundry dark shadows which haunted the gloom to the rear of him. Presently, his opportunity seemed to have come; he sprang noiselessly forward, and aimed a terrific blow at the dog's head, while Gregory Staines gripped Mr. Bootle's throat at the same moment to prevent him making an outcry ere the other man could despatch him.

But, somehow, everything went wrong. The dog eluded the assassin's blow, and, with a deep growl, sprang at his throat, the weight of his onslaught flinging the man to the ground. Simultaneously, the place seemed full of men, and ere Gregory Staines had time to realise what was happening, he had been knocked aside, and overpowered, to find himself, a few moments later, gagged, and bound hand and foot, in a vehicle that was rapidly being driven away from Lina. Beside him sat a stalwart young fellow, of soldierly bearing, who made it his business to tighten his bonds and gags, everytime that he struggled to free himself. Opposite him sat Sergeant-Major Twiley and Mr. Bootle, the former looking triumphant, the latter tremulously thankful.

"I reckon your gallop's stopped now, old man," remarked the sergeant-major. "You won't steal many more diamonds, or murder many more stewards, after this."

"Thank God that at last I have secured the real thief, and that Harley will soon be at liberty now," was Mr. Bootle's inward comment.

As for the prisoner, who knew that his fancied safety had been his ruin, and that his daring pursuer had kidnapped him, in order to convey him to English territory, where he would be amenable to the laws of England, he could only see one horrible object ahead of him—the gallows.

XXII

ANNIE'S RETURN

M r. Cory's residence was in a wonderful state of bustle and excitement. A telegram had been received from Annie to the effect that at last she had been successful in her mission, and that her captive was now on his way to England, under such efficient surveillance that he was not likely to escape again. There were endless conjectures as to how this desirable result had been brought about; but none of these were permitted to interfere with the active preparations that were being made, in order to give a fitting welcome to the girl whose courage and devotion had been crowned with such happy results. For no one doubted that now all would progress satisfactorily, and that such proofs of Harley's innocence would be forthcoming as would conduce to his speedy liberation.

There was only one blot on the general jubilation. That was the loss of Hilton, of which all his friends were convinced that Hugh Stavanger was the cause. Yet even Mrs. Riddell, bitterly as she grieved for him, felt thankful to God today. For was not the unmerited disgrace under which Harley languished a much sorer trial than even death itself? And had not at least one of her boys a happy future before him? As for Annie, she had ceased to look upon her as an ordinary mortal. For, she thought, no mere girl could have done what she had done, and come unscathed through her adventures.

"John, you are sure you did not mistake the time, and that you will not be too late to meet her?" inquired Miss Margaret anxiously.

"There is ample time, my dear," was the reply. "And even if I were too late, the child is well able to dispense with anybody's assistance, especially as she has Briny with her."

"I wouldn't be too sure of that. Now that the terrible strain is nearly over, a reaction may have set in, and the dear girl may be as helpless as a fashionable doll."

This reflection quickened Mr. Cory's movements, with the result that he was at the station quite an hour before the time appointed. He found the long wait almost intolerable, but at last received the reward he sought. Miss Margaret's conjecture had not been far wrong. True,

Annie was still quite capable of directing minor affairs, but the strain imposed by the necessity for daily, nay hourly, deception, had told upon her, and she looked both weary and ill. But she soon brightened up under her father's radiant welcome. Her return home was in every respect a joyful one, and the whole of the evening was spent in interchanging confidences and experiences.

The trio of elderly people listened with the greatest astonishment to Annie's account of her adventures in Lina, and of the mode in which Hugh Stavanger, alias Gregory Staines, had been kidnapped and conveyed to English territory. Considerable management and diplomacy had been required ere it had been possible to overcome certain difficulties in the way of securing his arrest and transshipment to England. But at last all was arranged, and the culprit would be put upon his trial for the suspected murder of Hilton Riddell.

"And how have matters progressed here?" Annie inquired at last. "You are all well, and you tell me, Dad, that Harley feels confident of success. I have been so fortunate myself that I cannot but hope you have also had some little gleams of enlightenment."

"And you are quite right, dear," exclaimed Miss Margaret, triumphantly. "There is no end of news to tell you. To begin with, old Mr. Stavanger—"

"No, that isn't the beginning of the story," interrupted Mr. Cory, smiling.

"Now, John, who is to tell the story—you or I?"

"Oh, you, of course."

"Then be good enough to let me tell it in my own way. I shall just start where I did before. Captain Cochrane—"

"Captain Cochrane? What of him, for Heaven's sake?" cried Annie, in great excitement.

"Did you ever try to tell anything to more unreasonable people, Mrs. Riddell? They want to hear all sorts of news, and yet they take the words out of my mouth."

So said Miss Margaret, and she did not feel at all sweet tempered as she said it. But Annie speedily smoothed her ruffled plumes, and then she continued without interruption: "Captain Gerard called to see us one evening, and explained a great deal that had transpired during his last voyage. As you are already aware, he also said that he had seen Captain Cochrane in London. You may be sure that we recommended a vigorous search, and only yesterday that search ended satisfactorily. Our man was discovered close to the house in which his sister lives, and was only captured after a very desperate resistance. Unfortunately for his future chances of defence, he at once conjectured the cause of his arrest, and protested that the passenger of the 'Merry Maid' was the only man to blame for the steward's disappearance. Even if this were true, though, he tacitly admitted himself to be an accessory to crime after the fact, and very plainly showed that he had regarded himself as liable to arrest on suspicion at any moment. Probably Hugh Stavanger may try to place the onus of guilt upon the captain. But, however this part of this long string of troubles turns out, there will be quite enough evidence elicited to prove that the diamond merchant's son left England with a great deal of the stolen property in his possession. Our solicitors have already moved for a new trial, and we have secured several important witnesses, Captain Gerard having been very helpful to us. His motives must be regarded as quite disinterested, too, for he has been promised the permanent command of the 'Merry Maid,' Captain Cochrane's resignation having been sent in. Your father saw this resignation at the office of the shipowners, to whom he had explained our whole story, but as there was no address of his on the document, it gave us no clue to the man's present whereabouts. He just seems to have hidden himself in obscure lodgings, and to have imagined that our pursuit of him would soon be abandoned. You are to see Harley tomorrow. He knows something of what has been going on, as we thought it cruel to refuse him a gleam of hope, now that things have progressed so well. I am not sure that he won't worship you, when he sees you."

But this prospect proved so overwhelming to the over-wrought girl that she burst into a passion of weeping, and hurried up to her own room. Mrs. Riddell found the sight of Annie's emotion unbearable, and also lost her composure, while Mr. Cory and Miss Margaret looked at each other in blank dismay.

"I think I must follow Annie upstairs," said the latter at last.

"By no means, my dear," objected Mr. Cory. "A cry will do the child good. Our presence would only impose restraint upon her. Depend upon it, she will come down soon, all the better for giving way for once. God knows she must have had nerves of iron lately, and it was high time that her work was done. She has borne up splendidly, but to have continued the strain under which she has lived since Harley was committed would have killed her."

And Mr. Cory was quite right. The girl had borne as much as she could. But she came back presently, quite composed, and ready to talk things over quietly. Mrs. Riddell had gone to bed, but, even after supper was over, Annie proved herself an insatiable listener.

"How is the Stavanger family going on?" she asked.

"Well," her father answered. "I rather think that Mr. David Stavanger must have become aware of his son's guilt, and that the effort to hide it is preying upon his mind. I hear that he has dissolved partnership with his brother, and has realised his share of the business. His eldest daughter is married, and he has gone with his wife and younger daughter to live at Boulogne. It has been an object with me to keep him in sight, as I thought it possible that his son might join him. The dissolution of partnership and the removal seem to have been very suddenly taken steps indeed, and my private inquiry agent told me that they were the result of a quarrel with Mr. Samuel Stavanger. If this is true, perhaps the latter suspects his nephew's guilt."

"Whether he does or not is immaterial to us, father. We can prove all that is necessary without him."

"Yes; but we could not be sure of that until lately. The capture of both the culprits was hardly to be hoped for. Come in!"

In response to this permission, a servant entered to say that Mr. Jenkins wished to see Mr. Cory. Mr. Jenkins, feeling sure of a welcome, followed the servant into the room, and was speedily communicating some important information to his three hearers.

"Annie," said Mr. Cory, as soon as the servant had closed the door behind her, "this is the agent who has been working for us at Boulogne. Perhaps he has some fresh discoveries to report."

"You are right, sir," said Jenkins, ensconcing himself comfortably on the seat pointed out to him, and basking in the warmth of the comfortable fire. "Mr. Stavanger had hardly reached Boulogne, when he developed symptoms of serious illness, and both doctor and nurses were speedily in requisition. Mrs. Stavanger pleaded indisposition on her own account, and declined to immure herself in a sick room. Hence her husband was entirely given up to strangers, for the little girl was of no use as a nurse. One of the women who has been engaged for this office is an Englishwoman, and she has proved singularly amenable to pecuniary persuasions. In a conversation which I secured with her yesterday, she gave me some extraordinary information. Mr. Stavanger's ailment, it appears, is brain fever, and his whole thoughts are centred upon various events connected with, and subsequent to, the diamond robbery. He raves incessantly of his son, and of all the trouble he has brought upon him. These ravings I have tried to arrange in their chronological order, and, always premising that they are not the mere phantoms of a diseased brain, I conclude them to reveal the following facts: Mr. Stavanger became convinced of his son's guilt, sometime not long before Mr. Riddell's committal. Certain indiscretions on the part of Hugh Stavanger caused others beside his father to learn of his guilt. One of these others was a servant named Wear, who at once proceeded to blackmail the family on the strength of her knowledge. This woman died very suddenly, and Mr. Stavanger has been haunted by a belief that his son compassed her death. You, I know, had an idea that the old gentleman himself had a hand in the affair. But whatever may be attributed to the son, I feel sure that the father was not to blame in this respect. Yet he was quite prepared to go to great lengths to shield his scapegrace son, and knowing him to be a thief, and suspecting him to be a murderer, he aided his escape from England in the ss. 'Merry Maid.' While staying at St. Ives, several weeks after this, he had an extraordinary find in the shape of a sealed bottle, containing papers. These papers appear to have been written and signed by Mr. Hilton Riddell, on board the 'Merry Maid,' before being sealed in the bottle and thrown into the sea. Their purport was a complete description of all that had taken place on board the vessel since it had sailed from London, and they evidently contained proof enough of Hugh Stavanger's guilt. If such a bottle was really cast into the sea, it was a very strange chance that threw it into the hands of the only man besides those denounced in it who could have a great personal interest in suppressing and destroying its contents."

"Extraordinary!" exclaimed Mr. Cory. "Why, it would have saved months of work and suspense for us. But—I am afraid it reveals only too truly what has been the fate of poor Hilton! He had penetrated the secrets of the villains, and felt that his life was not safe. They must in their turn have suspected him, and Stavanger and Cochrane had deemed it necessary to their safety to remove him. Oh, the scoundrels! But the poor lad shall be amply avenged!" Annie, too, was excited and indignant. So was Miss Margaret. But they forbore all interruptions, and Mr. Jenkins concluded his narrative in his own way.

"But little remains to be added," he said. "This Mr. Stavanger seems to be an odd mixture of bigotry, hypocrisy, and blind devotion to his disreputable son. He talks quite jubilantly about the opportune deaths of Mr. Edward Lyon, and of a man by whom he himself was being blackmailed because of the fellow's knowledge of Hugh Stavanger's guilt.

Then his ravings are to the effect that Harley Riddell must have really done something to make himself accused of God, since Providence is visibly fighting against him. He also seems to be aware of many of your abortive attempts to entrap his son, and the poor soul triumphs over you in his delirium. Here is the last of his speeches that have been reported to me. 'Yes, you may search the world over, but you will not discover Hugh. He is only the chosen instrument of Providence, used to bring his deserts to a villain who has committed some great and undiscovered crime. That villain's brother's would have betrayed Hugh, and what became of him—Bah! Neither he nor you can prove aught against my son—unless the sea gives up its dead!'"

XXIII and Last

JUBILATE

The Court was crowded in every part. For the trial of Hugh Stavanger and Captain Cochrane upon various indictments had aroused immense public interest, and countless rumours were afloat respecting the wonderful acumen, devotion, and heroism of Miss Annie Cory. She was inundated with applications for interviews, and greatly as she disliked much of the questioning to which she was subjected, she submitted to it with the best grace she could muster, for Harley's sake. Soon she found herself a popular idol. Her sayings and doings were recorded in every paper in the land that could obtain authentic information on the subject, and some of the more obscure journals that were endowed with smart editors determined to rescue them from their obscurity, published racy accounts of fictitious interviews with her, which were so extraordinarily full of favourable criticism that none but her enemies could have taken serious exception to them. She was photographed so often that at last she rebelled, and vowed that she would never enter a photographer's studio again. She figured as Miss Una Stratton, as Miss Cory, and as Mr. Bootle, her various presentments being so totally different that curiosity to see her rose to its highest pitch, and caused her every movement to be watched with the keenest interest. Briny, too, came in for his share of attention. For had it not transpired that his mistress in all probability owed her life to him? And that he was a cordially beloved member of the Cory family? Through the publication of his history a curious thing came to pass.

One day an elderly gentleman sought an interview with Mr. Cory. Briny was in the hall when he arrived, and welcomed him with the wildest demonstrations of affection. It transpired that Briny's original name had been Neptune; that his master's name was Woodstock; that the latter had been ordered by his doctors to do a little sea-voyaging; and that after going out to America, he had engaged a return passage for himself and his dog on board a timber-laden vessel bound for England, and not likely to make such a rapid passage as a steamer, his object being to spend a few weeks over the voyage.

"But things did not work quite so satisfactorily as had been expected," he continued. "Bad weather overtook us, after various incidents that I will not inflict upon you, and the day arrived when it was deemed necessary to take to the boats. I had the misfortune to receive a blow on the head that rendered me insensible for a time, and when I came round, I found, to my great grief, that my faithful friend Neptune had been left on board the wreck to perish in miserable solitude. I believe I was very violent in my denunciations of the inhumanity that could thus desert him. But even my partiality was at last convinced that, the boats being overcrowded already, there could have been no room found for a large dog, except at the risk of all our lives. As it was, one boat swamped and drowned its occupants. When, quite recently, I read of your brave action in saving the life of a deserted dog, I felt sure it must be dear old Neptune."

"But you won't take him away from us?" pleaded Miss Margaret, anxiously.

"My dear madam," quoth Mr. Woodstock, "do you take me for a heathen?"

But—will the disclosure be premature?—she was subsequently induced to take him "for better, for worse," and the pair are as happy and jolly as people who have been half a century in finding their affinity ought to be.

Annie had had an interview—nay, two interviews, with her lover, and had the satisfaction of leaving him more hopeful each time. Of course his love and gratitude knew no bounds, but we will spare the reader all his extravagant testimonials to his lady love's perfections, or his bitter denunciations of those who had brought about the necessity for her exceptional exertions.

"I think we may almost venture to pity them now," said Annie, gently. "They have been very wicked, and all their schemes have to some extent been successful. But their downfall has come at last. They cannot escape conviction, and this knowledge must in itself be a very bitter punishment for them. Your liberation is now only a mere matter of form, and all England is in sympathy with you, even before the trial which is to decide whether you and Hugh Stavanger are to change places or not."

"Our solicitor told me that Mr. Stavanger was supposed to be dying. Have you heard how he is?"

"He is recovering; but will never be the same man again. They say that his illness has changed him in many respects, and that he has vowed never to look upon his son again."

"I suppose he is a man of extreme views. Probably his present aversion to his son is more the result of the disgrace which it is no longer in his power to avert, than of a suddenly aroused conviction that his son has sinned against law and morality, or that, by swearing against me, he has helped to make me that son's scapegoat. I don't believe in after-discovery repentances. All the same, I believe he is to be pitied, and I shall bear no animosity."

"That is well spoken, Harley! The punishment of our enemies rests now with the law, and personal enmity may well die out. If only poor Hilton were alive there would be such complete happiness in store for us that our hearts need have no room for enmity."

Nevertheless, on the day of the trial Annie watched the progress of events with the keenest anxiety, and her distress of mind worried her friends considerably. Suppose her hopes were destined to be blighted, after all? Suppose the evidence at command should not prove enough, even yet, to bring about a reversal of the sentence which had weighed upon Harley for months? It was no wonder that she looked anxious, or that she was oblivious of everything but the actual progress of the trial. She was well supported by friends, who lavished every attention upon her that could be spared from the dear, sweet-faced old lady, to whom this day was of such awful moment. They had all tried to persuade Mrs. Riddell to remain at home, fearing that the excitement might be too much for her.

Their persuasions were most kindly meant. But the firmness with which they were resisted convinced them that they were also ill-judged. One of Mrs. Riddell's sons was to have his fate decided that day— either as a free man, or as a confirmed felon. And two men were to be arraigned for depriving her of her other son. It would be dreadful to look upon that son's murderers. But it would be intolerable anguish to remain at home in ignorance of what was being done.

Captain Cochrane and Hugh Stavanger both looked round with a feeble assumption of confidence when they were brought into the dock. But there were very few sympathetic looks to be seen on the sea of faces at which they gazed, and their eyes soon sought the ground, the one scowling angrily, and the other looking abjectly miserable.

No expense had been spared that could help to prove Harley innocent of the diamond robbery, even the Maltese jeweller being to the fore. Harley Riddell himself was strongly cross-examined, and his worn, haggard appearance caused his fond mother and faithful sweetheart

ELIZABETH BURGOYNE CORBETT

some additional sorrow. But as the trial progressed, excitement lent a colour to his cheeks and a brightness to his eyes which showed his friends how soon he would recover his former vigour when free, and proved to strangers how handsome he was likely to appear when happy.

The prisoners were on their trial, the one for the diamond-robbery, and the other for being accessory after the fact. On the morrow they were to take their trial for the suspected murder of Hilton Riddell. Somehow, however, the proofs which had been deemed so overwhelming by Harley's friends, did not appear as if they were going to be sufficient to compass the conviction of Hugh Stavanger for the robbery. There was plenty of proof that he had had a great many diamonds in his possession, and his evident desire to evade observation argued guilt on his part. But there was no one who could or would prove that the jewels in Hugh Stavanger's possession were the jewels that had been stolen. Both his father and his uncle had suddenly disappeared, and their evidence was unavailable. This disappearance confirmed everybody's moral conviction that Hugh Stavanger was guilty.

But moral conviction is not proof, and without proof no man may be judged. Accused's counsel began to be very hopeful. Presumably everything would have turned upon Hilton Riddell's evidence, and, curiously enough, the lack of evidence was likely not merely to fail in proving Stavanger's guilt, but to be the actual means of proving his innocence. It was fully explained why he had joined the "Merry Maid." But although he might have gained important evidence, he had not returned with it, and was, therefore, useless as a witness. It being impossible to prove that Mr. Hilton Riddell was possessed of any information likely to be detrimental to Mr. Hugh Stavanger or to Captain Cochrane, it naturally followed that a motive for his supposed murder was wanting. Given no motive, only absolute proof that the men had been seen to commit the murder would be sufficient to secure their committal upon the capital charge, and though all the world felt morally convinced of their guilt, the men had capital counsel who knew, none better, how to make black look like white, and whose professional reputation was staked upon the winning of such a desperate looking case.

There was also a certain judge on the bench with whom the words "justice" and "moral conviction" became obsolete terms as soon as he entered upon the study of "law." He also prided himself upon his ability to enforce the dictates of law in all their naked severity, in spite of all the clamourings of public opinion. Nay, public opinion was his especial bugbear, and his judicial eye always rested with particular disfavour upon anyone unfortunate enough to be deemed a popular favourite. He had read all about Annie's adventures, and had at once dubbed her in his own mind an unwomanly schemer. He didn't like unwomanly women. They set a bad example to others. Therefore an example must be made of them, and they must be shown that the dictum of one of her Majesty's judges cannot be lightly upset. Poor man! He was but human, and he could hardly be expected to view with favour an attempt to upset the judgment he had himself given when Harley Riddell was tried for the diamond robbery. Do not mistake me, dear reader, our noble judge would sacrifice his own private feelings if law bade him do so. But law must be paramount, and if law was ever doubtful, it must always consider itself opposed to sentimentalism and unwarranted interference.

Thus it happened that, by the enforcement of this enactment or of that, all the cherished proofs of Harley's innocence and Hugh Stavanger's guilt were ruthlessly torn to shreds, and more than one heart was turning sick with disappointment, when a strange commotion was heard among the crowd of people at the entrance of the court. There were loud cries of "Silence in Court." But these cries were unheeded. Indeed, the commotion waxed louder and became momentarily more irrepressible, as a man pushed his way through the crowd, while his name flew before him.

It was Hilton Riddell!

Hilton Riddell was that day a name to conjure with, and even the judge himself permitted his mind to entertain emotions that were not strictly of a legal tendency. But how describe the joy and delight of the mother who had pictured him lying dead at the bottom of the sea? Of the brother who thought that for his sake he had perished? Of the friends who now saw light ahead for Harley? Or the dismay of the two scoundrels who, though they were freed from the weight of bloodguiltiness, yet saw condemnation in store for them as the result of the evidence of this man, who had been given up by the sea for their undoing?

All this happened sometime ago. And our friends may be supposed to have settled down to the freedom and joy which is theirs. But even yet they cannot think calmly of the events of that wonderful day when blind justice seemed to be balancing her scales against them again, and when Hilton's opportune return wrought the condemnation of villainy, and re-united every member of a now happy family. Hugh Stavanger has ample time now in which to contemplate the fate he so ruthlessly inflicted upon another. And Captain Cochrane often laments the day that cupidity stole such a sorry march upon him.

Miss Una Stratton and Mr. Ernest Bootle have been relegated to the phantoms of the past, and even Miss Annie Cory has been merged into Mrs. Harley Riddell. Her husband has quite recovered his former health and good looks, though he is perhaps of a more serious disposition than of yore. He does not care to lead an idle life, but is at the head of a lucrative business established for him by his father-in-law. Needless to say, the said father-in-law did not care to be parted from his daughter, and the three live very happily together.

Hilton Riddell makes his mother's heart happy by his devotion to her, and she has no fear that the day will come when he will crave for the exclusive society of a companion of his own years. He also has embarked in a line of business which ensures him freedom from pecuniary anxiety.

Mr. and Mrs. Woodstock live next door to the house in which Mr. and Mrs. Harley Riddell and Mr. Cory reside, and it is questionable which of the homes Briny claims as his own.

Mr. and Mrs. Twiley, and Mrs. Dollman (on her marriage to a worthy young friend of the sergeant-major) received some very handsome presents from the Corys, and Hilton Riddell is not likely to forget all he owes to a certain worthy Captain Quaco Pereiro and his steward.

THE END

A Note About the Author

Elizabeth Burgoyne Corbett (1846–1930) was an English novelist, journalist, and feminist. In addition to her work for the *Newcastle Daily Chronicle*, Corbett was a popular adventure and detective writer whose work appeared in some of the Victorian era's leading magazines and periodicals. In response to Mrs. Humphrey Ward's "An Appeal Against Female Suffrage," published in *The Nineteenth Century* in 1889, Corbett wrote *New Amazonia: A Foretaste of the Future* (1889), a feminist utopian novel set in a futuristic Ireland. Despite publishing a dozen novels and two collections of short fiction, Corbett—who was once described by *Hearth and Home* as a master of the detective novel alongside Arthur Conan Doyle—remains largely unheard of by scholars and readers today.

A Note from the Publisher

Spanning many genres, from non-fiction essays to literature classics to children's books and lyric poetry, Mint Edition books showcase the master works of our time in a modern new package. The text is freshly typeset, is clean and easy to read, and features a new note about the author in each volume. Many books also include exclusive new introductory material. Every book boasts a striking new cover, which makes it as appropriate for collecting as it is for gift giving. Mint Edition books are only printed when a reader orders them, so natural resources are not wasted. We're proud that our books are never manufactured in excess and exist only in the exact quantity they need to be read and enjoyed. To learn more and view our library, go to minteditionbooks.com

bookfinity & MINT EDITIONS

Enjoy more of your favorite classics with Bookfinity,
a new search and discovery experience for readers.
With Bookfinity, you can discover more vintage
literature for your collection, find your Reader Type,
track books you've read or want to read,
and add reviews to your favorite books.
Visit www.bookfinity.com, and click on
Take the Quiz to get started.

Don't forget to follow us
@bookfinityofficial and @mint_editions